Robert Cooper Seaton

Sir Hudson Lowe and Napoleon

Robert Cooper Seaton

Sir Hudson Lowe and Napoleon

ISBN/EAN: 9783337350024

Printed in Europe, USA, Canada, Australia, Japan

Cover: Foto ©Andreas Hilbeck / pixelio.de

More available books at **www.hansebooks.com**

SIR HUDSON LOWE

(From a Pencil Drawing in possession of his Daughter)

SIR HUDSON LOWE
AND NAPOLEON

BY

R. C. SEATON

LONDON

DAVID NUTT, 270–271, STRAND

1898

PREFACE

The following pages contain some matter hitherto unpublished. Miss C. M. S. Lowe, the only surviving daughter of Sir Hudson Lowe, has also kindly allowed me the use of a few letters and other documents. The portrait of Sir Hudson Lowe is from a pencil drawing, in the possession of Miss Lowe, made in 1832.

R. C. S.

CONTENTS

Sir Hudson Lowe and Napoleon

CHAPTER I

THE QUESTION STATED

THE character and career of Napoleon form a subject of perennial interest. He has already taken his place beside Mary of Scotland and Oliver Cromwell, and some other historical personages about whom, after all is said, the most diverse opinions are held. But we never get to the end of Napoleon. Fresh volumes about his life or portions of it are continually appearing. Not long ago we had from the practised hand of Mr. T. P.

O'Connor a book exhibiting Napoleon from many different points of view, both of friends and of enemies. A little earlier came *Napoléon et les Femmes* from M. Frédéric Masson, a professed worshipper. Mr. Baring-Gould has lately brought out a new *Life*, and the monumental work of Professor Sloane is just completed. No apology therefore is necessary for an attempt to clear the character of one whose name is indissolubly connected with the closing scenes of the Emperor's life, of one who has been so maligned and calumniated that his name has become a byword for peevishness of temper, coarseness of language, and petty persecution. It is scarcely necessary to say that I refer to Sir Hudson Lowe, the Governor of St. Helena during Napoleon's captivity. French national pride has made it a point of patriotism to cling to charges long after they have been disproved, but

2

something different might have been ex
pected from ourselves. Sir Hudson Lowe
makes no demand on our generosity; he
claims only justice, and it is hard that now
that he has been more than half a century
in his grave this claim should not be
accorded to his memory. Soon after the
death of Napoleon, a small but noisy
group, aided by political interest, party
spite, and the specious statements of a
lying book, captured the ear of the public
to listen to their version of the treatment
of the Emperor at St. Helena, and they
have more or less kept it ever since. A
few months before the death of Sir Hudson
Lowe a writer in the *United Service
Magazine*, in October 1843, thus expressed
himself: "So complete a reaction has
taken place, in this country at least, that
it may now be doubted whether any man
of information and reflection can be found
to countenance opinions unfavourable to

Sir Hudson Lowe." There are, however, a good many such to be found even now. No man, it is true, "of information and reflection," much less an historian, ought to entertain such opinions, but there is considerable excuse to be made for the British public. When people have once had it instilled into their mind that some atrocious deeds have been done, they do not rest content (and all honour to them for the feeling) till they have seen punishment inflicted for the wrongdoing. But they are not so careful about getting hold of the real culprit. If they make some one serve as an expiatory sacrifice their virtue is apt to be satisfied. This was the case here. They first admitted without sufficient ground that Napoleon had been ill-used, and then, finding it was possible to make a victim of Sir Hudson Lowe, they promptly sent him into the wilderness to bear the sins of the British Government as well as his own, both equally imaginary. There is little similarity between Sir Hudson Lowe and Lord Byron, yet they have this in common, that both, though for very different reasons, have been made scapegoats to save the character of the nation. Byron was offered up to vindicate our domestic virtue, Sir Hudson Lowe to expiate our supposed sins against Napoleon. There is also the difference that Byron was guilty, while Sir Hudson Lowe was innocent; but of both the remark of Macaulay on Byron holds good: "He is a sort of whipping-boy, by whose vicarious agonies all the other transgressors of the same class are, it is supposed, sufficiently chastised. . . At length our anger is satisfied. Our victim is ruined and heartbroken. And our virtue goes quietly to sleep for seven years more." Not only the public ear but also the literature of the day, and more especially that of France, became so saturated with the notion of Napoleon as a victim to the petty malevolence of his so-called "jailer" and "executioner" that people almost forgot there was another side to the question. And they had the good excuse that Sir Hudson Lowe himself had never spoken out when he might have done so with effect : a fatal mistake for which he paid the penalty to the day of his death. The reason why he thus acted will be dealt with later on. It was not till the publication of the *History of the Captivity of Napoleon at St. Helena*, by the late Mr. William Forsyth, Q.C., nine years after the death of Sir Hudson Lowe, that a full statement was made on the other side. His character is there completely vindicated, it is true, but it is also completely buried. It is unreasonable to expect the average reader to work his way through three thick volumes weighted with numerous official documents. The materials are only too ample, the vindication is only too complete. What was wanted was a small book setting out the salient facts in reasonable compass. The three volumes, though admirably written, are rather a storehouse from which the necessary proofs may be drawn. It is true the book has made a certain impression on the public. It is no longer possible to speak of Sir Hudson Lowe with the same licence of abuse as was heard previously ; but, while it is allowed that " he was not a bad man," he is still charged with harshness of temper, want of courtesy, violence of language and vacillation of purpose. But, if Forsyth's book had made the impression that it ought to have made, it would have been impossible for a respectable firm to have republished, even with certain omissions, O'Meara's *A Voice from St. Helena.* I have been speaking of the public only. For the professed student or the historian, after Forsyth's book, to persist in offensive charges against Sir Hudson Lowe is scarcely creditable. It may be admitted that he was occasionally wanting in tact, but with that exception the charges that are still made against him show either that certain writers have not read Forsyth's book with sufficient care, or that they have closed their eyes to the plainest evidence. More than forty years ago Mr. Forsyth wrote : "The historian has charged him (Sir Hudson Lowe) with meanness and cruelty, and the satirist has turned him into ridicule. He has been painted as a man whose conduct and language befitted the turnkey of a gaol rather than a British officer intrusted with the execution of a duty of unparalleled delicacy and importance. And even those who have duly estimated the difficulty of his task, and suspected the veracity of his assailants, have been unable to divest themselves of an uneasy consciousness that he might have performed his duty in a more gracious manner. The tone of their defence has been rather that of apology than vindication. And for this I cannot but think that Sir Hudson has himself been in some degree to blame. When we consider the ample materials he possessed for refuting his enemies and putting the libellers to shame, we cannot but marvel that he should have allowed the grave to close over him without having published his defence to the world."* These words are almost as true now as when they were written. One honourable exception must be made in favour of the writer of the notice on Sir Hudson Lowe in the *Dictionary of National*

* *History of the Captivity of Napoleon at St. Helena,* i. 122, 123.

Biography. He has done justice to the good intentions and excellent performance of duty by the Governor of St. Helena.

One French writer — Lamartine — has had the good sense and moral courage to run counter to the prepossessions of his fellow-countrymen in the following remarkable words : " In reading with attention the correspondence and notes exchanged on every pretext between the attendants on Napoleon and Sir Hudson Lowe, one is confounded at the insults, the provocations, and the invectives with which the captive and his friends outraged the Governor at every turn. Napoleon at that time sought to excite by cries of pain the pity of the English Parliament, and to furnish a grievance to the speakers of the opposition against the Ministry, in order to obtain a removal nearer to Europe. The desire of provoking insults by insult, and of afterwards exhibiting these insults as crimes to the indignation of the Continent is plainly evident in all these letters." *

In days past Sir Hudson Lowe has been, as Forsyth puts it, a *bête-noire* of the French imagination; but Truth, it is said, is the daughter of Time, and I have written the following pages in the hope that the fair-minded Frenchman and the average Englishman may now be disposed to regard the events at St. Helena in the dry light of historical fact. In any case, to do justice to the memory of Sir Hudson Lowe can cast no aspersion on the reputation of Napoleon.

* *Histoire de la Restauration*, vi. 416.

CHAPTER II

BEFORE ST. HELENA

HUDSON LOWE, only son of John Hudson Lowe, surgeon of the 50th Regiment of Foot, was born at Galway in 1769, a year remarkable for the birth of Napoleon himself and several others connected with his history. The Duke of Wellington, Marshals Ney and Soult, and Lord Castlereagh were all born in this year. He was educated at Salisbury School, and in the eighteenth year of his age received a commission in the regiment of which his father was still surgeon. At this time it was stationed at Gibraltar, and there young Hudson Lowe remained till 1792. He now obtained leave of absence and travelled through Italy, which gave him the opportunity of acquiring a thorough knowledge of Italian—a knowledge which was of much use to him in after life. To this he afterwards added Spanish and Portuguese. His first service was on the expedition to Corsica under Sir David Dundas. In 1795 he received a Captain's commission and was appointed Deputy Judge-Advocate in Elba. Next he served in Portugal under Sir C. Stuart, and was sent to Minorca to take charge of a corps of Corsicans then being raised. Captain Lowe took part in the Egyptian Expedition, and, with the temporary rank of Major, commanded the Corsicans from Minorca who formed part of the reserve under Sir John Moore. "The vigilance and method with which he conducted outpost duty," says the writer of the Memoir of Sir Hudson Lowe in the *United Service*

Magazine,* "was conspicuous and procured a pointed eulogium from General
Moore. 'Lowe,' were his words, 'when
you're at the outposts I always feel sure
of a good night's rest.'" Of the Corsican
corps and its commander, Sir Robert
Wilson writes as follows in his *History
of the British Expedition to Egypt*: "This
corps in every action, and especially in the
landing, distinguished itself particularly,
and Major Lowe, who commanded it,
gained always the highest approbation.
Indeed, it was a corps which from its
conduct and appearance excited general
admiration, and did honour to the nation
of the First Consul of France."

After the peace of Amiens Major Lowe
was appointed to the 7th Fusiliers, and
shortly afterwards one of the perma-
nent Assistant Quartermasters-General.
General Sir John Moore remained his

* April 1844, p. 593.

firm friend, and as it is rightly considered a distinction *laudari a laudato
viro*, to be praised by one whom others
praise, one of several letters to Major
Lowe may be quoted here :—

"CHATHAM, 21*st April*, 1802.

"MY DEAR LOWE,—I congratulate you most
sincerely on your appointment to the Fusiliers.
It is nothing more than you well deserve; and
if I have been at all instrumental in bringing it
about I shall think the better of myself for it.
I hope before we leave that the Fusiliers will be
at home, and in a way to be actively employed.
I trust you will always consider me as a person
warmly interested in your welfare, and that you
will let me hear from you occasionally; and if
duty or pleasure bring you near me, now or hereafter, you may depend upon the best reception I
can give.—Believe me, very sincerely and faithfully,   "JOHN MOORE."

When the peace proved to be hollow,
Major Lowe was selected by the Government, in July 1803, to proceed on a secret
mission to Portugal in order to inspect the

troops and fortresses along the frontier, and report on the practicability of defending the country by united British and Portuguese forces. On the termination of this mission he was employed to raise the regiment of Royal Corsican Rangers, of which he was appointed Lieut.-Col. Commandant, and, taking part in the expedition to Naples under Sir James Craig, made frequent journeys to Naples and Sicily. In June 1806 Lowe was placed by Sir John Stuart (who had succeeded Sir James Craig) in command of the island of Capri, which had lately been captured by Sir Sidney Smith. Here he remained with five companies of the Corsican Rangers as a garrison, which was subsequently strengthened by the remainder of the Corsicans and the Maltese regiment. Soon after his arrival at Capri, Colonel Lowe showed his humanity by addressing a letter of remonstrance to General Berthier, then chief of the staff of the French army in Naples, in which he appealed to him to put a stop to the numerous military executions in Calabria. For more than two years Colonel Lowe was Governor at Capri, until, in October 1808, the island was attacked by a powerful French naval and military expedition from Naples, and, after a siege of thirteen days, compelled to surrender, chiefly owing to the misconduct of the Maltese regiment and the want of naval assistance. Colonel Lowe, however, refused to come to any other terms than those of a free evacuation with arms and baggage—terms which were after some difficulty accorded. It is true that Sir William Napier, in his *History of the Peninsular War*, says that it was at Capri "Sir Hudson Lowe first became known to history, by losing in a few days a post that, without any pretensions to ability, might have been defended for as many years."

Sir Hudson Lowe and Napoleon

We cannot be surprised that the enemies of Sir Hudson Lowe have eagerly seized on this unfortunate remark of the illustrious historian, for unfortunate and unjust it is, and it is a sufficient reply to say that officers at the time and near the spot, who had every opportunity of judging, expressed a very different opinion. Thus, Major-General Lord Forbes wrote to Colonel Lowe: "I am convinced that Sir John Stuart will take an early opportunity of expressing to you, as well as to the public, the sense he entertains of the unremitting zeal, ability, and judgment which your conduct has displayed under your late trying circumstances at Capri," and Sir John Stuart himself, the Commander-in-Chief, wrote: "I am happy to express my perfect satisfaction at your own able, gallant, and judicious conduct, as well as at the zealous and animated support which you acknowledge to have received from your officers and those brave soldiers who adhered to and returned with you hither in the defence of the town of Capri : a point which, after your first most unexpected and unaccountable disaster at Ana Capri, could scarcely any longer be regarded as a military post." It has also been represented that the garrison consisted of 2000 men and the French assailants of 1200 ; the fact being that the garrison, exclusive of officers, was 1361 men, while the French were between 3000 and 4000.

In 1809, under the chief command of Sir John Stuart, Colonel Lowe with his Corsicans formed part of the force that captured the islands of Ischia and Procida, and Lowe made the capitulation of Ischia with the French general, by which the garrison was forced to surrender as prisoners of war. In the same year Colonel Lowe was appointed second in command on the expedition to the Ionian

Isles, and conducted the landing on Zante, after which Cephalonia and Cerigo surrendered. General Oswald, who was in command of the military forces, appointed Lowe to be Governor in Cephalonia, "certain that so delicate a trust could not be reposed in more able hands."* He continued to administer the civil government of Cephalonia, with which Ithaca was soon afterwards united, during the end of 1809 and the beginning of 1810. Colonel Lowe then urged on General Oswald the advisability of securing the island of Santa Maura, which contained a strong fortress and was in immediate proximity to the coast. The expedition was successfully carried out and Colonel Lowe was thanked three times in the public despatches. The island of Santa Maura was then added to the civil government of Cephalonia and Ithaca, and for two years Colonel Lowe

* Despatch, October 5, 1809.

administered it without special remuneration. He prepared a report on the island for the Colonial Office, and on his departure was presented by the grateful inhabitants with an address of thanks and a gold sabre. Lowe returned home in February, 1812, on leave, having lately obtained the rank of full colonel. He says : " I was then in my twenty-fourth year of service, and had never been absent a single day from my public duty since the commencement of the war in 1793. I had been in England only once during that time, and then only for a period of six months during the peace of Amiens."

Colonel Lowe was already known to Government as an active, vigilant, and trustworthy officer, especially fitted for foreign missions on account of his knowledge of languages, when at the beginning of 1813 he was appointed to a position in which his talents could be displayed on a larger scale. In January he was sent on a secret mission to the north of Europe to inspect the Russian-German legion, a body raised principally from the deserters and prisoners of the contingents impressed by Napoleon into his Russian campaign. Lowe went first to Sweden and saw Bernadotte, then Prince Royal, at Stockholm. From here he crossed the Gulf of Bothnia on the ice, and joined Lord Cathcart, the British Ambassador to Russia, at the Emperor Alexander's headquarters at Kalisch in Poland, where he quite won the confidence of that monarch. In May he joined the headquarters of the Allies and was present at the battle of Bautzen, on which occasion he had his first view of Napoleon. Lowe was next ordered to inspect the whole of the Hanoverian and German forces in British pay, and was sent by Lieutenant-General Lord Stewart to join the Russian and Prussian army under

Field-Marshal Blücher. Thus he happened to be present at the battle of Leipsic. Next he was summoned for another tour of inspection in the north of Germany, and in January 1814 ordered to rejoin Blücher's army during the campaign in France. As the only English officer of rank with this army, Colonel Lowe's position was one of great importance and responsibility, and General Stewart compliments him on the clearness and detailed nature of his despatches. In this capacity he was present with the Prussian army in thirteen general engagements. When the fighting was over Colonel Lowe was the officer selected to bring to England the news of the abdication of Napoleon and capitulation of Paris, for which service he received the honour of knighthood. The Prussian Order of Military Merit followed him home, and on his return to Paris the Emperor Alexander conferred on him the

Russian Order of St. George. He was also made a K.C.B. and promoted in June to the rank of Major-General. During the summer General Lowe was appointed Quartermaster-General of the army in the Netherlands, and was required to inspect and report on the state of the fortresses to be established as a barrier against France. Colonel Basil Jackson —afterwards an intimate friend of Sir Hudson Lowe and at this time a very young officer on the Staff—thus speaks of his first acquaintance with him : " About this time Sir Hudson Lowe was appointed Quartermaster-General, succeeding Colonel, afterwards Lord, Cathcart. . . . His successor proved to be all we could desire, as an active, diligent, and accomplished officer, who not only worked hard himself but also kept his officers on the alert, evincing towards them at the same time the utmost consideration."* In September, Sir Hudson Lowe had occasion to write to General Count Gneisenau, the chief of Blücher's Staff, an officer whose admirable talents are too well known to need any encomium. Count Gneisenau had long been a warm friend of Sir Hudson Lowe, and in his reply begins with the following strong expressions of regard—the original is in French : "It is with the greatest satisfaction, my very dear and honoured General, that I have received your letter of the 15th of September, which tells me that you have still preserved the remembrance of a man who is infinitely attached to you, and who in the course of a memorable campaign, if there ever were one, has learnt to appreciate your rare military talents, your profound judgment on the great operations of war, and your imperturbable *sang-froid* in the day of battle. These rare qualities and your

* *Waterloo and St. Helena*, p. 7.

honourable character will link me to you eternally." Again, if I may anticipate a little, I am tempted to quote a passage from a letter by the same writer to Sir Hudson at St. Helena, in October 1817, which well expresses the general confidence felt on the Continent in the vigilance of the Governor—I translate again from the French : " Thousands of times have I carried my thoughts over that vast ocean solitude to that interesting rock on which you are the guardian of the public repose of Europe. On your vigilance and on your force of character depends our safety ; if you were to relax your rigorous care against the wiliest villain in the world,* if you were to allow your subordinates to grant him any favours through a mistaken pity, our repose would be compromised, and honest folks in Europe would be a prey to their old anxiety. I have often

* *Le plus rusé scélérat du monde.*

been questioned on this point—I who was known to have the honour of your acquaintance—and I always replied that I could guarantee your loyalty, your sagacity, and your vigilance. The most devoted of your friends, I am so deeply interested in your well being that I beg you across the sea to have the goodness to give me news of your health, your pleasures, your pains, your domestic happiness, in short of all that can interest a friend." As we shall see, however, Sir Hudson Lowe showed, in fact, much more leniency to Napoleon than Count Gneisenau would have approved. Field-Marshal Blücher also wrote to Sir Hudson Lowe, in January 1815, as follows : " The recollection of a man whom, during so very memorable an epoch as the last campaign, we have learnt to esteem and respect, remains dear to us, and will be ever dearly valued through life. On such grounds you may rely with confidence on the continuance of my attachment and friendship. I wish you joy from my heart on the important post which the Prince Regent, in his confidence, has bestowed upon you, and I rejoice that the choice has fallen upon a man so perfectly equal to fulfil the duties of it in its whole extent."

Sir Hudson Lowe was still Quartermaster-General in the Netherlands when Napoleon landed from Elba in March 1815, the Prince of Orange being then, as before, Commander-in-Chief. The position of Sir Hudson Lowe was now one of the highest importance, and he soon had an opportunity of rendering a signal service to his country, and indeed to Europe. By the authority of the Prince of Orange, he had despatched a letter to the Prussian headquarters urging that their army should be assembled on the Meuse, in a situation where it would be ready to co-operate with the British in the defence of Belgium. Accordingly, in spite of the opposition of General Müffling, chief of the Staff, the Prussian army proceeded to carry out this suggestion. But now, for political reasons, the Prince of Orange and his father the King of Holland drew back, and were desirous of keeping the Prussian army behind the Meuse. "The Prince of Orange directed me," says Sir Hudson Lowe, in a letter written from St. Helena to Lord Bathurst, "to write to General Kleist or General Müffling accordingly. I told the Prince that, having been the means of making these arrangements with the Prussian army, by which it was approaching to act in concert with the British, I did not feel I could with propriety now write to propose a different plan of operation. The Prince, however, insisted upon the necessity of my writing, saying that the instructions he had received from the

King were positive. I then used every argument in my power to convince the Prince, that, as a *military measure*, it was the only one by which the Low Countries could then be saved, that to propose anything contrary would be entirely against my own opinion as the Quartermaster-General of the Army ; and finding he still persevered in desiring me to write, I was compelled at last to say to him that I could not consider the determination which had been taken as founded in any reasons of a *military nature*, and that if they were the result of *political considerations* they were not of my competence to write upon ; I therefore begged that he would allow me to decline being the medium of communication." It is perhaps not too much to say that the firmness of Sir Hudson Lowe on this occasion enabled part of the Prussian army to be present at Waterloo. It is pleasing to

record that subsequently the Prince of
Orange admitted the correctness of Sir
Hudson Lowe's judgment, and some
twenty years later, when King of Holland, greeted him most warmly at a levée
of William IV.

In April the Duke of Wellington arrived
to take command of the allied army, and in
the beginning of May Sir Hudson Lowe
was appointed to the command of a body
of English troops to act with the British
squadron under Lord Exmouth on the
south coast of France. Sir Hudson Lowe
was succeeded as Quartermaster-General
by that gallant soldier Colonel Sir William
Howe De Lancey, who was struck by a
cannon-ball at Waterloo and died a few
days later.* Sir Hudson Lowe afterwards
married Colonel De Lancey's sister, the

* Of him the Duke of Wellington wrote in a despatch :
" The death of this officer is a serious loss to myself and
to His Majesty's service."

widow of Lieutenant-Colonel William Johnson. The duties of the British forces in the south of France turned out to be very light. Marseilles was at once occupied without opposition, and Toulon yielded to the Royalists on Sir Hudson's approach. The conduct of Sir Hudson Lowe procured for him the warm esteem of the distinguished Admiral with whom he had co-operated. "You have, my dear Sir Hudson," writes Lord Exmouth under the date of August 27, 1815, from Marseilles, "my entire esteem and regard, and I am sensible, had opportunity been afforded us for more brilliant services, that we should have woven our confidence into the most perfect and lasting friendship." The letter ends with these words: "God bless you, Sir Hudson; may health, success, and happiness attend you! Believe me ever, your sincerely and faithfully attached friend, Exmouth." The Municipal Council of Marseilles, it may be mentioned, testified their respect for his conduct during the occupation by voting to him, as well as to Lord Exmouth, a handsome piece of silver plate. On August 1, while at Marseilles, Sir Hudson Lowe received a notification that he was appointed Governor of St. Helena, with the local rank of Lieutenant-General, to have the charge of the person of Napoleon, who had about a fortnight previously taken refuge on board the *Bellerophon*.

I have been somewhat minute in tracing the earlier career of Sir Hudson Lowe, because, in view of what followed, it is important to keep in mind the public services he had rendered and the reputation which he bore up to this time. In his *Life of Napoleon*, Lockhart says of Sir Hudson Lowe that the utmost that could be said against him was that his " ante-

c

cedents were not splendid." This is not
putting the matter fairly. One usually
confines the word "splendid" to services
which are in themselves exceptionally conspicuous, or which are rendered so by the
high rank or position of the person who
performs them. In this sense the services
of Sir Hudson Lowe were not "splendid,"
nor could they have been so from the
nature of the case; but they may be
described as most valuable and distinguished services, and such as had repeatedly earned the commendation of
Government. I could have quoted many
other letters from officers whose merit is
well known, all testifying to the high
esteem felt for Sir Hudson Lowe; but
those which I have already given are
perhaps sufficient.

It is more to the point to observe that,
although it has often been said that Sir
Hudson Lowe was not an officer of suffi-

ciently high rank or distinguished career
to be entrusted with the custody of
Napoleon, this was by no means the
opinion of Napoleon himself until he
had quarrelled with the Governor. In a
well-known letter to Sir Hudson Lowe,
dated December 19, 1816, Count Las
Cases writes as follows—and on this particular point it suited him at the moment
to speak the truth : " 'A man is appointed
to take the command here,' we said (you,
sir, were the person alluded to), 'who
holds a distinguished rank in the army ;
he owes his fortune to his personal merit ;
his life has been passed in diplomatic
missions at the headquarters of the
Sovereigns of the Continent, where the
name, the rank, the power, the titles of
the Emperor Napoleon must have become
familiar to him.' . . . . ' This man,' we
said, 'in his diplomatic career will have
formed just notions both with respect to

persons and things. His arrival alone is
therefore a sufficient pledge of the favourable nature of his instructions with respect
to us.' '*Did you not tell me,*' said the
Emperor to us one day, '*that he was at
Champaubert and at Montmirail? We
have then probably exchanged a few cannon-
balls together, and that is always, in my
eyes, a noble relation to stand in.*' Such
was the disposition in which Sir Hudson
Lowe was expected." No doubt it is
here the object of Las Cases to contrast
the expectations they had formed of
Sir Hudson Lowe with the reality which
(according to their view) they experienced,
but these words are conclusive testimony to
the *nature* of those expectations. Again,
Napoleon said to Colonel Sir George
Bingham, who commanded the troops at
St. Helena, when he heard of the arrival
of Sir Hudson Lowe: "I am glad of it;
I am tired of the Admiral (Sir George

Cockburn),* and there are many points I should like to talk over with Sir Hudson Lowe. He is a soldier and has served ; he was with Blücher ; besides, he commanded the Corsican regiment and knows many of my friends and acquaintances."† Let us then hear no more of this ; if Napoleon was satisfied with the antecedents of Sir Hudson Lowe, surely no one else has a right to complain of them.

The character borne by Sir Hudson Lowe up to this date may be fairly summed up in the words of Colonel Basil Jackson, who wrote a short " tribute to his memory " just after his death :

"I was honoured with the friendly notice of Sir Hudson Lowe, and enjoyed much of his

* Rear-Admiral Sir George Cockburn took Napoleon to St. Helena on the *Northumberland*, and was entrusted with his safe custody until the arrival of Sir Hudson Lowe.

† From a letter of Sir George Bingham to Sir Hudson Lowe.

confidence during a course of thirty years. I knew him when his military reputation marked him as an officer of the highest promise; I witnessed his able conduct as Governor of St. Helena; I saw him when the malice of his enemies had gained the ascendant, and covered him with unmerited opprobrium; I beheld him on his deathbed: and throughout these various phases of his career I admired and respected his character, while I truly loved the man. I knew him to be a kind, indulgent, affectionate husband and parent, a warm and steady friend, a placable, nay, generous enemy, and an upright public servant." *

This is a testimonial of which any man might be proud, and if Sir Hudson Lowe had died on the day he was appointed Governor of St. Helena the sentiments here expressed would have been received with universal applause. And yet we are asked to believe, on the authority of Mr. Barry O'Meara and some of Napoleon's fellow-exiles, that the character of Sir

* *United Service Magazine*, March 1844, p. 417.

Before St. Helena

Hudson Lowe was as nearly as possible the reverse of all this! That he was mean, jealous, suspicious, tyrannical, utterly wanting in kindness and courtesy, fit only to be a jailer or a hangman! No one, as Juvenal says, ever became base in a moment; and surely, before a shred of evidence is heard on one side or the other, we have here a psychological puzzle of no ordinary difficulty.

CHAPTER III

AT ST. HELENA

A GREAT mass of literature has accumulated round the events of Napoleon's exile at St. Helena, and it would be a hopeless task to attempt to deal with it in detail, or with all the charges that have been brought against Sir Hudson Lowe. I must therefore select a few of the most striking, and point out how easily they can be refuted. What is really difficult is to clear away the dense clouds of prejudice and misrepresentation that still envelop the memory of Sir Hudson Lowe and all that concerns him. However, before dealing with the evidence, such as it is, it is necessary to consider the circumstances altogether, and the aims and objects of those on whose testimony Sir Hudson Lowe has been condemned.

To select an officer upon whom should be laid the responsibility for the safe custody of Napoleon was no easy matter for the British Government, and that they appointed Sir Hudson Lowe shows the high opinion they had formed of his vigilance, conscientiousness, and general ability. I am by no means claiming that he was exempt from faults, and these faults I will endeavour to state later ; but, whatever his faults were, they were not those that have been generally attributed to him. It may be said fearlessly that the choice of Government was fully justified by the conduct of Sir Hudson Lowe in his arduous position, and that the unmerited obloquy cast upon him, and still clinging to his memory in the minds of many people, was mainly the result of the efficient manner in which he carried out his trust. As he repeatedly said, the office was not one that he had sought; but when once it was offered to him he had too high a sense of duty to decline it. Sir Hudson Lowe had, as we have seen, high qualifications for the post. On the other hand, it cannot be denied that the service he had seen had happened to be such that the new Governor could scarcely be regarded by Napoleon as a *persona grata*, and of this the Emperor was not slow to remind him. For instance, Sir Hudson Lowe had been in command of the Corsican Rangers, a body of men whom Napoleon not unnaturally regarded as brigands and traitors to their country. He had at the close of the war received the submission of Toulon, the place from which at the beginning of the war Napoleon had driven the British, and where he had first made his mark as a military genius. Again, as we have seen, Sir Hudson Lowe had brought home the news of Napoleon's abdication, and had been knighted for that very service. All these circumstances were certainly personal arguments against the appointment of Sir Hudson Lowe.

Napoleon always contended that he gave himself up only as the guest of the British nation, and he claimed their hospitality as such. He therefore regarded it as an act of tyranny and injustice that he should be treated as a prisoner of war. But this view cannot bear inspection for a moment. Napoleon in fact had no option but to surrender, if he wished to escape a worse fate. There was no hope for him. If he was still to live he might take one of three courses. He might have put himself at the head of the army at the Loire for a short period (but only to be killed or captured); he might have let himself be made prisoner; or he might have surrendered to one or other of his foes. The last course, the one which he actually adopted, was also the best for himself. He afterwards said he regretted he had not surrendered to the Emperor of Russia or the Emperor of Austria. Very probably he did have this regret. We cannot of course say what would have happened in that case, but he would scarcely have surrendered to the King of Prussia, for Blücher had publicly declared that he would have had him shot over the grave of the Duc d'Enghien. It was idle then to pretend that he came as a guest on board the *Bellerophon.* The circumstances were very different from what they were a year before, when Napoleon had been allowed to take the sovereignty of Elba. He had returned to France, and it was now evident that no terms could bind him. Savary and Las Cases did all they could to induce Captain Maitland, of the *Bellerophon,* to receive Napoleon as the guest of the British nation ;

but that officer declined, as a matter of course, to enter into any engagement for his Government, and simply undertook to convey him safely to England. At a subsequent period Las Cases himself admitted this. At that time Napoleon was not regarded with the sentimental interest which now attaches to his name and fate. There was hardly a household in the United Kingdom that could not point to the loss of some one at least of its members through the long continuance of the Great War. In a celebrated passage Livy describes the dream of Hannibal: "So he looked and saw behind him a monstrous serpent moving forwards, while trees and houses fell crashing before it; storm and a peal of thunder followed. Then, as he asked in wonder what the monstrous form portended, he heard a voice say: 'Thou seest the desolation of Italy; go onwards on thy way; cast no look behind, nor question further, nor try to draw the fates from their obscurity.'"* On the track of Napoleon followed the desolation of Europe, and Shelley's lines, on hearing the news of his death, are no exaggeration :

"Ay, alive and still bold," muttered Earth,
  "Napoleon's fierce spirit rolled
In terror, and blood, and gold,
  A torrent of ruin to death from his birth.
Leave the millions who follow to mould
  The metal before it be cold,
And weave into his shame, which like the dead
Shrouds me, the hopes that from his glory fled."

At the time of Napoleon's surrender, an exile to St. Helena or elsewhere was considered very lenient treatment, for there was then, as Sir Walter Scott reminds us, a considerable party in England who were in favour of handing him over to the Government of Louis XVIII. It is true that the Opposition in Parliament professed

* Livy, xxi. 22.

46

a horror at the measure dealt out to Napoleon, but that was merely because they were the Opposition ; and if they had been in power they could hardly have resisted the will of the nation, which demanded some measure of the sort, and readily acquiesced in the banishment to St. Helena. When then Napoleon considered it an outrage that he should be banished to St. Helena at all, the personality of the Governor was a minor matter. As Las Cases wrote in a suppressed passage of his Journal : "The details of St. Helena are unimportant : to be there at all is the great grievance."*

The conduct of Napoleon and his suite towards Sir Hudson Lowe was not due merely to caprice or ill-temper, but was the result of a carefully-settled plan by which they hoped to secure their object,

* "Les détails de Ste. Hélène sont peu de chose ; c'est d'y être qui est la grande affaire."

and that object was the Emperor's recall.
For a long time they confidently expected
this, either through some revolution in
France, or even from a mere change of
Government in England. Thus, on the
fourth interview of Sir Hudson Lowe
with Napoleon, the latter said, in reply
to some question about a house: "In a
couple of years there will be a change
in the Ministry in England, or a new
Government in France, and I shall no
longer be here." Napoleon evidently
over-estimated the difference between the
Government and the Opposition in the
English Parliament. He thought that
the speeches of the Opposition, merely
made with the view of embarrassing their
opponents, really expressed their con-
victions, and that if Lord Holland and
his friends came into power he would
speedily be recalled from exile, for almost
from the first the treatment of Napoleon,

like most other things, was made a party question. In accordance with this deliberate plan it was necessary that Napoleon and his grievances should be put before the European, and more especially the British, public, at any cost. "It was his business to have complaints," says Lockhart. The favourite Napoleonic maxim, "Policy justifies everything," was constantly in request at St. Helena, and the disciples did not fall far short of their master in its application.

"In pursuance of this system," says a writer in the *Hereford Journal*, in 1853, probably Colonel Jackson, "all communications from Sir Hudson, written or otherwise, were to be misunderstood; points which it was well known to be out of the power of Sir Hudson to concede were to be perpetually insisted on ; all acts of courtesy were to be construed into insults, every proposed amelioration of their condition was to be received as an aggravation of their misery, while lying to any extent was to be unscrupulously resorted to whenever it could forward the great end they had in view." Generals Bertrand, Montholon, and Gourgaud, and Count Las Cases were all honourable men—"at least according to the *Code Napoléon*," as Colonel Jackson caustically observes—and we need not bestow too much severity of censure on any of their acts in the service of a master whose will to them was law. Count Las Cases was a worshipper by nature : he said the Emperor was his god, and an eloquent French writer has said of him, " He had the servility of a domestic and the blindness of a devotee." Bertrand was, according to Mr. Henry,* who knew him well at St. Helena, the most honest and honourable man of the Longwood estab-

* *Events of a Military Life*, vol. ii. p. 92.

lishment, and, he adds, "*on all other subjects than those immediately relating to the Emperor's interests*, of unimpeachable veracity." This, however, is rather a large deduction, considering that Bertrand said or did little at St. Helena that had not reference to the Emperor. Even among this party Count Montholon was distinguished for his disregard of truth, and Napoleon himself cautioned him against this habit. An amusing instance of this is found in the statement in his *Récits** of his regret at General Gourgaud's departure, when only a month before Gourgaud had challenged Montholon to a duel, which the latter declined only on the ground of his attendance on the Emperor! Of General Gourgaud I

* Vol. iii. p. 3 (English edition). See also Forsyth, ii. 248 and iii. 390. The date of the challenge was Feb. 4, 1818, and General Gourgaud embarked for England on March 14. As a favour he was allowed to sail for Europe direct instead of going first to the Cape.

shall have more to say later. While at St. Helena he conducted himself with perfect propriety, which was probably one reason why he fell into the Emperor's bad graces. The evidence of the French, then, is of little account as against Sir Hudson Lowe; but their admissions are valuable as evidence in his favour. Now it happens that we have these admissions in abundance. When Las Cases was sent away from St. Helena for misconduct, at the end of 1816, the MS. of his journal came into the hands of the Governor, who, before returning it, very properly had it copied as a matter of public interest. This journal contains many passages that are suppressed in the journal as published. One of the suppressed passages is as follows:

"We are possessed of moral arms only; and in order to make the most advantageous use of these it was necessary to reduce into *a system* our demeanour, our words, our sentiments, *even our privations*, in order that we might thereby excite a lively interest in a large portion of the population of Europe, and that the Oppositior in England might not fail to attack the Ministry on the violence of their conduct towards us." *

Colonel Basil Jackson informs us that† while visiting Paris in 1828 he accidentally met Count Montholon, who invited his wife and himself to pass a few days at his country seat. Colonel Jackson thus continues :

"He (Count Montholon) enlarged upon what he termed *la politique de Longwood*, spoke not unkindly of Sir Hudson Lowe, allowing he had a difficult task to execute, *since an angel from heaven as Governor could not have pleased them.* When I more than hinted that nothing could justify detraction and departure from truth in carrying out a policy, he merely shrugged his shoulders and reiterated, 'C'était notre politique,

---

* Under the date of November 30, 1815. This passage is given by Forsyth, vol. i. p. 5.

† *Waterloo and St. Helena*, pp. 103, foll.

et que voulez-vous?' That he and the others respected Sir Hudson Lowe I had not the shadow of a doubt; nay, in a conversation with Montholon at St. Helena, when speaking of the Governor, he observed that Sir Hudson was an officer who would always have distinguished employment, as all governments were glad of the services of a man of his calibre. Happening to mention that, owing to his inability to find an officer who could understand and speak French, the Governor was disposed to employ me as orderly officer at Longwood, Montholon said it was well for me that I was not appointed to the post, as they did not want a person in that capacity who could understand them; in fact, he said, 'We should have found means to get rid of you, and perhaps ruined you.' Now, it was simply because an officer of the rank of captain had always acted at Longwood, and the Governor knew that to have sent them an officer who was only a lieutenant would have been deemed a kind of insult by Napoleon, and as such resented. I was subsequently glad the project failed."

These admissions require no comment. Moreover, we have the evidence of

O'Meara, who, writing to Sir Thomas Reade* on July 10, 1816, while he was still on good terms with Sir Hudson Lowe, thus expresses himself: "They [the French] are sufficiently malignant to impute all these things [want of proper provisions] to the Governor, instead of setting them down as being owing to the neglect or carelessness of some of Balcombe's [the purveyor] people. Every little circumstance is carried directly to Bonaparte, with every aggravation that malignity and falsehood can suggest to evil-disposed and cankered minds."† It is needless to add that this passage does not occur in his published book.

We thus have a clue to guide us through all the plausible statements made by writers on behalf of Napoleon. There

* The Deputy Adjutant-General. A French publication called him *Le Castlereagh de Ste. Hélène.*

† Forsyth, i. 237.

was a regular series of them. First, the publication of Warden, the surgeon of the *Northumberland*, then that of Santini, one of Napoleon's servants. Both these appeared in the Emperor's lifetime, and we have the advantage of his own comments on them. Of Warden's book he said: "The foundation of it is true; but in it there are *cento coglioniere e cento bugie* (a hundred absurdities and a hundred lies)." But this is speaking too gently. General Gourgaud wrote of it as a "mere tissue of falsehoods." Of Santini's book (which, as it turned out, was not by Santini at all) Napoleon said that it was "a foolish production, exaggerated, full of *coglioniere* and some lies." However, these *brochures* served their purpose, which was to gull the British public. Las Cases' journal is of course a more serious publication; but the published journal, as above remarked, is

very different from the MS. journal that
came into the hands of Sir Hudson Lowe.
Other publications were the *Récits* of
Montholon, and especially *A Voice from
St. Helena* of O'Meara, of which I must
speak more particularly. There seems to
have been no personal animosity on the
part of the French towards Sir Hudson
Lowe. Like Lady Teazle, they took
away his character with the utmost good-
nature. This is shown, not only by their
own admissions afterwards, but also by
their conduct immediately after the death
of Napoleon. "The hatchet was buried,"
and Counts Bertrand and Montholon (Las
Cases and Gourgaud having left St.
Helena long before) made their peace
with Sir Hudson Lowe, who, with his
accustomed generosity, was quite willing
to meet them. They all called at the
Governor's house, stayed to lunch, and
all dined there on the following day.

There was no reason for keeping up appearances any longer. We have similar testimony from Colonel Jackson, who wrote thus to Mr. Forsyth: "I never heard any of the French say a word against Sir Hudson Lowe's bearing towards them. His orders to his officers were to do all that courtesy and kindness could dictate to render the situation of the French persons as little unpleasant as possible, and, so far as I saw, every desire on their part was promptly attended to. He was himself a man possessing little of what is called *manner*—no man had less of that—but he was full of kindness, liberality and consideration for the feelings of others." Thus we find Madame Bertrand returning thanks for a donkey which the Governor sent for her little boy, and for a picture in tapestry which had been detained from her by a person in the island, and which the Governor instantly procured for her. " These are trifles in themselves," says Mr. Forsyth, " but they are trifles which indicate kindness; and a man's disposition and character are often more clearly shown in little things than in matters of more serious import." From this absence of personal feeling I am afraid I must except Count Las Cases, who certainly seems to have cherished some spite against Sir Hudson Lowe. At any rate, his son did, as we shall see later. For some time before his death Napoleon himself, perceiving that his hopes of recall were entirely baseless, seems to have become more reconciled to his lot, and really to have shown some gratitude for the constant attentions shown him by Sir Hudson Lowe. On his deathbed he charged Bertrand and Montholon to seek a reconciliation with the Governor, which was done with the result above mentioned. The tragi-comedy of five years was played out.

It must be allowed that Napoleon was less difficult to deal with than his attendants. Affairs might have been more readily adjusted if more personal intercourse be-tween the Governor and his illustrious captive had taken place. But they only had five interviews in all,* and the last of them was only four months after Sir Hudson Lowe's arrival. It was, as we have seen, Bertrand, Montholon, and others who persistently and purposely exaggerated and misrepresented every-thing, in order to make occasions of quarrel. This was, in short, *la politique de Longwood.*

The complaints of the French writers are such as might be expected from the

* I do not here include the short interview of June 20, 1816, which was merely for the purpose of introducing to Napoleon the new admiral, Sir Pulteney Malcolm.

circumstances in which they were placed, and naturally, owing to those circumstances, would not make much impression on an impartial reader. Moreover, their own admissions have sufficiently discounted the value of their evidence. There is another person whose statements and insinuations have been the chief cause in England of the odium cast upon Sir Hudson Lowe. I refer to Napoleon's surgeon, Mr. Barry O'Meara. We have seen what manner of man Sir Hudson Lowe was. Let us also examine the character of Mr. Barry O'Meara, and when that is fully appreciated the most difficult part of my task will be accomplished. One cannot be surprised at the amount of prejudice raised against Sir Hudson Lowe by *A Voice from St. Helena.* It is written with an engaging air of frankness—"an affected candour," says Colonel Jackson—and considerable literary skill, and would naturally lead the reader into the belief of the account given therein. Besides this it seemed unlikely, to say the least, that a British officer would so far forget his position and his duty as to enlist himself secretly in Napoleon's service, to become *l'homme de l'Empereur*, as the phrase was, and therefore to misstate facts deliberately for the purpose of producing sympathy for Napoleon. And again, if a British officer were willing to be guilty of such treachery, there did not seem to be sufficient inducement for it. But these two unlikely things turned out to be strictly true. O'Meara was guilty of this baseness, he had sufficient inducement, and he received the reward which he had certainly earned. Barry O'Meara was surgeon on board the *Bellerophon* when Napoleon surrendered to Captain Maitland. He recommended himself to the Emperor's notice, and was subsequently asked to become his surgeon.

At St. Helena

It is not necessary to suppose, in the first instance, anything further than that O'Meara succumbed to the fascination of the Emperor. There is abundant testimony to the great personal attraction which Napoleon exercised over those with whom he came into contact. How great this attraction was may be inferred from a remark of Admiral Lord Keith, who in reply to repeated applications on behalf of Napoleon for a personal interview with the Prince Regent exclaimed : " That would never do ! In half an hour they would be excellent friends ! "

As the Emperor's surgeon, O'Meara sailed to St. Helena on board the *Northumberland*, and was in personal attendance upon Napoleon afterwards until his summary removal by the order of the Government in the summer of 1818. Being a man of plausibility and considerable social gifts, he managed for some time to keep on good terms both with Napoleon and with Sir Hudson Lowe, and *spontaneously* gave to the latter a good deal of information of how matters were going at Longwood. The Governor, in fact, got his salary raised from £365 to £520. Sir Hudson Lowe, however, was naturally unwilling to question O'Meara on this delicate subject, as it might be thought he wished the surgeon to act as a spy—until he ascertained that O'Meara was in the habit of carrying on a detailed correspondence with a friend at the Admiralty, and then he considered that what was of sufficient importance to be conveyed direct to England for the benefit of the Cabinet—for this correspondence was shown to them— certainly ought to be communicated to himself. Even then the Governor left it to O'Meara to say what he chose, and to select what was proper to be thus communicated. And yet O'Meara had the

astounding impudence to charge the
Governor with wishing to employ him as
a spy! This charge against Sir Hudson
Lowe has unfortunately met with much
belief. For instance, the writer of the
notice of O'Meara in the *Dictionary of
National Biography* says : " Lowe wished
him to act to some extent as a spy upon
his prisoner and to repeat to him the
private conversation of the Emperor."
We have only O'Meara's bare word for
this, as against documentary evidence with
which it is inconsistent. Let us hear also
Sir Hudson himself. In a private letter
to Lord Bathurst soon after O'Meara's
enforced departure, the Governor entered
into the question of his conduct towards
that person. He said : " There are three
points upon which I have conceived Mr.
O'Meara may endeavour to raise a voice
in his favour.

"*First*, he may say I wanted to employ

him as a spy. *Answer:* I never asked him to give me any other information than what he had been in the habit of carrying to Sir George Cockburn, and this I asked him even in Sir George's presence ; since when even Count Montholon has acknowledged I had a right to expect being informed of any discussions into which he might enter with General Bonaparte respecting my duties or his own, or of any improper communications going on.

" *Secondly*, he may ask why, if I had complaints against him, I did not bring them to a hearing. *Answer:* The complaints against him were of such a nature as that, if proved, I could not have suffered him to remain on the island without the worst effect of example, from a supposed impunity, upon the officers and inhabitants in general ; and having received his resignation, reporting to Government General

Bonaparte's application for a French or Italian physician to succeed him, I considered it best, unless he should himself apply to the Admiral, to let matters rest until the answer of Government should be received. [That is, an answer to a representation made by Sir Hudson Lowe about Mr. O'Meara's conduct.]

"*Thirdly*, he may complain of my general mode of treatment towards him. *Answer:* If, through consideration to the very particular circumstances of General Bonaparte's situation, I was induced to act with a moderation and apparent lenity towards Mr. O'Meara which I could not have done towards any other individual, this was no reason I should at the same time continue to him those personal regards as an officer and a gentleman which his conduct and proceedings had appeared to me to destroy all claim to. I never, therefore, suffered him to enter my house, except by the outer door of it, which leads to the Secretary's office; and whenever he attempted to manifest any impertinence in his replies to my interrogatories, dismissed him immediately from my presence." It is not pleasant to be told to leave the room, and after reading "thirdly" we can hardly be surprised that O'Meara cherished some animosity towards Sir Hudson Lowe.

But O'Meara was not only untrue to his salt, he was guilty of a double treachery, for at the very time when he was giving some information to Sir Hudson Lowe and much more to his friend at the Admiralty (Mr. Finlaison) he had actually long been under a pledge to Napoleon himself "not to reveal the conversations that passed between them, unless they related to his escape." Mr. O'Meara, having already made shipwreck of his own honour, tried to induce others to follow his example. I have already had occasion to refer to Mr. Walter Henry, who was at this time at St. Helena as assistant-surgeon, and soon as acting surgeon, of the 66th Regiment. In his very interesting work, *Events of a Military Life*, he devotes about one hundred pages to his experiences on the island. Not a word has ever been uttered against his character or impartiality, and his narrative is amply confirmed in its details by the letters and official documents which Mr. Forsyth has published. Mr. Henry gives an account of how an attempt was made to bribe him to become *l'homme de l'Empereur* through the agency of O'Meara. He had attended Cipriani, the *maître d'hôtel* of Napoleon, during an illness which proved fatal, and he was asked through O'Meara to accept a breakfast service of plate. He describes in an amusing way the visions he had of this present, but the British Parliament had lately made the acceptance of any gift from Napoleon a criminal act, and his duty was clear. " The matter," he says, " was plain enough—a palpable attempt at a bribe, to enlist even so humble a person as myself into Napoleon's service, and to bind him down to implicit obedience, by first making him commit himself in a wrong action." It was a case of this sort, another attempt to bribe in which O'Meara acted the part of an intermediary, that led to restrictions being laid on him by the Governor in April 1818. However, the account of Mr. Forsyth is much too lengthy and minute, so I will quote the narrative of Mr. Henry, every word of which is amply confirmed by documentary evidence.

" Mr. O'Meara, on finding his intrigues with the persons he had tried to bribe discovered, sent in his resignation; whilst at the same time Napoleon applied for a foreign medical attendant. Sir Hudson Lowe sent home their applications, confining Mr. O'Meara to the bounds of Longwood, and placing him under the same restrictions as the other persons of Napoleon's household. A few weeks after this an order arrived from England to send home Mr. O'Meara ; not from any representations from Sir Hudson Lowe, for there was not time for the recent offence of this gentleman to be communicated, but in consequence of information received by the Government at home inculpating him as the tool of the fallen Emperor." *

This information related to clandestine correspondence, and had been given by General Gourgaud, who had recently returned from St. Helena. It is important to observe that it was the Government and not Sir Hudson Lowe who removed Mr. O'Meara. Sir Hudson Lowe had not had up to this time proof of O'Meara's complicity, and the way in which the latter was backed up by influential members of the Government had prevented the Governor from taking all the steps he might other-

* Henry, ii, pp. 40, 41.

wise have taken. However, very soon after O'Meara's departure there arrived at St. Helena such convincing proof of his being a tool of the Emperor as amply justified the Government in their action. After April 1818, but before the summary order for O'Meara's dismissal had been received, O'Meara was excluded from the mess of the 66th Regiment, of which he had been an honorary member. Of course he has set this down entirely to the machinations of the wicked Governor. In his book he attributes it to Sir Hudson Lowe having employed Sir Thomas Reade to fill the mind of Colonel Lascelles with the most insidious calumnies against him, and to insinuate that his expulsion would be very agreeable to the Governor. As this is a good example of O'Meara's misrepresentations, I will give the particulars of it from the narrative of Mr. Henry, who was in a position to know accurately what happened. It is true that O'Meara was excluded from the mess, that it was due to the intervention of Sir Hudson Lowe, and that some of the officers of the mess did express their regret at his departure. However, let us hear Mr. Henry, and we can then judge whether Mr. O'Meara had much ground for complaint. He writes as follows :

"About this time Mr. O'Meara, having been discovered tampering with two or three individuals on the island, with the object of prevailing on them to accept presents clandestinely from Napoleon, in violation of the regulations in force; and being also accused of repeating the confidential conversation of our mess, of which he was an honorary member, at Longwood, the Governor stated the facts of the case to Sir George Bingham and the Commanding Officer of the 66th, intimating to the latter his opinion that Mr. O'Meara should not be permitted to continue a member of the mess, he having abused the privileges his position gave him. . . . Without consulting the officers of the mess, or submitting for their consideration the facts com-

Sir Hudson Lowe and Napoleon

municated to him by the Governor, the Commanding Officer sent a written intimation to Mr.
O'Meara that his society was no longer desired
by the regiment, which pretty strong hint the
doctor disregarded, came to dinner the same
day, and afterwards appealed to the officers of
the mess as to the propriety of his conduct
whilst mixing with them. Having been kept in
the dark as to the real culpability of Mr.
O'Meara, and being, perhaps, a little piqued at
the proceedings of their Commanding Officer,
they readily certified to the gentlemanly deport-
ment of Mr. O'Meara whilst he was a member of
the mess. . . . It is, I think, much to be
regretted that the officers of the 66th should
have given Mr. O'Meara any written certificate
of good conduct whilst a member of their mess.
However correct his behaviour might have been
before, the gross insult to our Commanding
Officer, and indirectly to ourselves, of sitting
down to dinner after the prohibitory note he had
received ought to have prevented any verbal or
written testimony being given to a man who
could act with such effrontery. As it turned out,
our certificate eventually became one chief prop
to the credibility of O'Meara's *Voice from St.
Helena*—a specious but sophistical book, full
of misrepresentations, yet more remarkable for

74

the *suppressio veri* than the *assertio falsi.* .
With reference to the breach of social confidence
in reporting our mess conversation to Bonaparte,
I have no doubt whatever of the fact. In the
unreserve of conversation with Madame Bertrand
on the voyage to England, after the death of
Napoleon, she acknowledged to me that this
charge was true." *

Immediately after his arrival in England
O'Meara addressed a long letter to the
Admiralty in self-justification, full of complaints against Sir Hudson Lowe. However, he overreached himself, and, intending
murder, committed suicide, for he introduced into it the monstrous insinuation
that the Governor had sounded him as
to his willingness to hasten the death of
the Emperor by artificial means.† The

* Henry, ii. pp. 40, 41.

† On this alleged design to poison Napoleon, Count
Montholon made a characteristic remark: "We don't
believe it ourselves, *but it is always well to say so.*" (Nous
ne le croyons pas nous-mêmes, *mais c'est toujours bon à
dire*). The malignity of the charge is hardly greater
than its absurdity.—Forsyth, iii. 187, note.

reply from the Secretary to the Admiralty
was short and obvious. It contained these
words :

"There is one passage in your said letter of
such a nature as to supersede the necessity of
animadverting upon any other parts of it. This
passage is as follows [the passage containing the
above insinuation is then set out]. It is impossible to doubt the meaning which this
passage was intended to convey, and my Lords
can as little doubt that the insinuation is a
calumnious falsehood; but if it were true, and
if so horrible a suggestion were made to you
directly or indirectly, it was your bounden duty
not to have lost a moment in communicating it
to the Admiral on the spot, or to the Secretary
of State, or to their Lordships.

"An overture so monstrous in itself, and so
deeply involving not merely the personal character of the Governor, but the honour of the
nation and the important interests committed to
his charge, should not have been reserved in
your own breast for two years, to be produced
at last, not (as it would appear) from a sense of
public duty, but in futherance of your personal
hostility against the Governor.

At St. Helena

" Either the charge is in the last degree false
and calumnious, or you can have no possible
excuse for having hitherto suppressed it. In
either case, and without adverting to the general
tenor of your conduct as stated in your letter,
my Lords consider you to be an improper
person to continue in His Majesty's service, and
they have directed your name to be erased from
the list of Naval Surgeons accordingly.—I have,
&c.   (Signed)   " J. W. CROKER."

This then is the man whose *A Voice
from St. Helena* has recently been republished !   This is the man who has been
immortalised by Byron in the well-known
couplet—

" And the stiff surgeon who maintained his cause
  Hath lost his place and gained the world's applause."

Of which two lines it is sufficient to say
that they contain about as much truth as
O'Meara's own statements.   The dismissal
of course put an end to O'Meara's public
career ; but if his activity was limited in
one direction, there were other fields open.

He could still calumniate, and his efforts
in this direction, we must admit, were
crowned with well-deserved success. In
1822 he brought out in two volumes, *A
Voice from St. Helena*—a book with an
attractive title, an agreeable style, and the
other characteristics I have before mentioned. It had an immense literary success,
five editions being run through in a few
months. What caused its popularity was
not the report of Napoleon's conversations
but the unscrupulous attack upon Sir
Hudson Lowe, for the literature of detraction has ever proved the most interesting.
Tacitus tells us that he deliberately began
his *Annals* with the principate of Tiberius,
in order to depict the Roman Empire in
the blackest colours. If I may compare
small things with great, O'Meara dipped
his pen in gall to show to us Sir Hudson
Lowe—the Tiberius of St. Helena—and
he has had his reward. Has he not been

embalmed in a couplet? Was he not pensioned by the Bonaparte family, admitted
to the affections of a rich old lady as a
third husband (her first marriage was nine
years before the birth of O'Meara), and
again pensioned by her, besides being,
as Mr. Henry says, "admired, quoted,
and panegyrised by all the Bonapartists
yet extant"? Is not this enough to
atone for the brutality of a dozen Sir
Hudson Lowes? And yet the writer of
the memoir of O'Meara—prefixed to the
recent edition of his book—speaks of his
"disappointed hopes"! Really, he must
have been hard to please. One result of
O'Meara's popularity among the Bonapartists, however, must not be omitted. It is a
remarkable example of the irony of human
life.

After the establishment of the Second
Empire, the mother of that excellent and
pious lady, the late Miss Kathleen O'Meara,

the authoress of the *Life of Ozanam*, and
many charming works of fiction, was, it
seems, awarded a handsome pension on
the ground of being the daughter-in-law
of that self-convicted calumniator, Mr.
Barry O'Meara! I say "self-convicted,"
for it is a singular fact in connection
with the exile of Napoleon at St. Helena
that most of the charges made against
Sir Hudson Lowe can be disproved by
the evidence of the very people who
made them. What supplies the poison
also supplies the antidote. We have
seen how Napoleon's suite admitted that
the whole of their conduct was based
on a system, and when that system necessarily came to an end on the death of
Napoleon they acknowledged they had
nothing to say against the Governor. So
in the case of O'Meara. He was carrying
on a correspondence with his friend Mr.
Finlaison at the Admiralty, and the garbled

accounts after wards concocted for *A Voice from St. Helena* are often in point blank contradiction to the accounts written at the time when the events narrated took place! It has been the business of Mr. Forsyth in his work to go minutely into this, and to confront O'Meara in page after page of his book with his own statements made in letters at the time. If ever any one spoke with a "double voice" it was O'Meara, but there has never been the slightest difficulty in deciding to which of the two we should give credit. O'Meara's character was thoroughly exposed in the *Quarterly Review* for October 1822, and to this O'Meara had the prudence not to make any reply. A few years after the death of Sir Hudson Lowe, Mr. Murray commissioned Sir Harris Nicolas, the well-known antiquary to prepare for publication the papers of the late Governor of St. Helena. Unfortunately, Sir Harris

Nicolas died before completing his task, but the opinion he had formed of some of the persons involved is expressed in two letters to Colonel Jackson, who had furnished him with some information. He thus writes from Boulogne, March 1, 1848, of Sir Hudson Lowe : " Not a spot will, I hope and believe, rest upon his memory. Such an exposure of lying malignity and scoundrelism on the part of O'Meara, Montholon, Las Cases, Antommarchi [the Italian surgeon], &c., as the work will exhibit, will be almost unprecedented." And again, on March 30, 1848 : " By the time I have finished I think I shall have been in company with *more liars* than any living author. If people meet in the next world with a know-ledge of each other, and with an exposure of their several falsehoods and villany, what must have been the scenes between Sir Hudson Lowe, Las Cases, and

O'Meara!"* The papers of Sir Hudson Lowe were subsequently put into the hands of Mr. Forsyth, who thus, in his preface, comments with just severity upon O'Meara :

> "I am not one of those who think that conduct such as he has been guilty of in slandering others may be sufficiently censured in the dulcet tones of gentle animadversion. He merits a sterner and more fearless judgment. Such writers are the pest of literature. They corrupt the stream of history by poisoning its fountains, and the effect of his work has been to mislead all succeeding authors and perpetuate a tale of falsehood."

He says further on, of O'Meara's book : "The object of the *Voice* was to avenge himself upon Sir Hudson Lowe, as the supposed author of his disgrace. And the means of accomplishing this was not difficult to a man who was content to sacrifice

---

* These letters are printed by Col. Basil Jackson in *Waterloo and St. Helena*, pp. 116, 117.

truth, honour, and honesty in the attempt.
He had been in constant intercourse with
Napoleon, and had had many confidential
interviews with Sir Hudson Lowe. He
knew perfectly well the real character of
every alleged grievance and complaint, and
he had taken copious notes of transactions
and conversations as they occurred. What
then was more easy than to recast these
memoranda and garble them to suit the
object he had in view—to suppress some
passages and add others, so as to alter the
tone and complexion of the original, and
yet preserve throughout a substratum of
fact? And this is what O'Meara has
done. It is a serious charge to bring
against a writer, and one which ought not
to be lightly made nor readily believed.
But, happily for the cause of truth, in
this case, proofs, amounting to demon-
stration, of what is here asserted can be
supplied."

At St. Helena

Mr. Forsyth then refers to the series of confidential letters of O'Meara to Mr. Finlaison and to the notes of conversations made at the time by Major Gorrequer, the Governor's Military Secretary. Of Napoleon, Mr. Forsyth says in his preface : " If I know anything of myself, my sympathies were in his favour. I cannot now sufficiently express my admiration of his genius ; but neither can I blind myself to the fact that he did not exhibit in misfortune that magnanimity without which there is no real greatness, and that he concentrated the energies of his mighty intellect on the ignoble task of insulting the Governor of St. Helena and manufacturing a case of hardship and oppression for himself. I have endeavoured to hold the balance even, and it is not the weight of prejudice, but of facts, which has made one of the scales preponderate." Of Sir Hudson Lowe he writes : " I was not asked to make out a case for Sir Hudson Lowe, nor, had I been asked to do so, would I have consented. I regarded the duty of examining the papers left by him as a solemn trust, for the due and truthful discharge of which I was responsible to the public, and a still more searching tribunal, my own conscience."

I have already described the nature of *A Voice from St. Helena.* I would gladly omit all mention of the republication in 1888, but as that book would now be given to any one inquiring for O'Meara's narrative, it is necessary to say a few words about it. It is handsomely got up, with excellent paper and print and some interesting illustrations, and has been rechristened *Napoleon at St. Helena.* There are some additions and some omissions. The additional matter shows all the good intention of O'Meara without his literary ability. The book is introduced with a quotation (given twice over) from Carlyle, who says : "O'Meara's work has increased my respect for Napoleon," and then goes on to compare Napoleon to Prometheus Vinctus, "arising above it all by the stern force of his own unconquerable spirit." Unconscious satire could hardly go further. Carlyle, after all, merely says (but expresses better) what any man who had read O'Meara's book *only* might say. It is obvious that he knew nothing of the other side, and in any case this *obiter dictum* cannot increase one's respect for the "Sage of Chelsea." Next come two short memoirs of Sir Hudson Lowe and Mr. O'Meara respectively, then a lengthy introduction. The writer on Sir Hudson Lowe, in the *Dictionary of National Biography*, to whom reference has already been made, shortly says of the "Lives" in this book that they are "worthless," an epithet which

87

an examination amply confirms. Taking them with the introduction, it is not unjust to say that many of the "facts" are fiction, while the method of argument shows an ineptitude of which O'Meara (to do him justice) would have been ashamed. One or two specimens will suffice. We read, in allusion to Sir Hudson Lowe's delay in prosecuting O'Meara for libel, "The only reason given by Lowe for his delay was the time required for meeting charges in which truth was so artfully blended with falsehood—an admission that we have a good deal of truth in the journal." Precisely: it is the truth mingled with the falsehood that makes it so dangerous. Exaggeration and misrepresentation of facts are always more difficult to expose than pure fiction, and a book that spreads these broadcast is proportionately more venomous and deadly, for

"The lie that is half a truth is ever the blackest of lies."

Again, there is quoted, as a testimonial
to O'Meara, an extract from a letter of
Lord Dudley (in the Dudley Letters) to
which he is certainly welcome. Having
met the author of the *Voice from St.
Helena* at dinner, Lord Dudley writes as
follows : " He is cheerful, good-humoured
and communicative, and, in spite of an air
of confident vulgarity which is diffused
over all his behaviour, the impression he
made on me was rather favourable. At
least my belief in what he has told was
strengthened by having seen him, and still
more so by some conversation which I
happened to have the very next day with
Sir G—— C——, whom I met at Gloucester
Lodge. He defends Sir Hudson Lowe
only just as far as prudence and decorum
oblige an official man to do so. Indeed,
he acknowledged that, with respect to
what passed in St. Helena, he was disposed
to take O'Meara's part. He mentioned a

circumstance, however, since O'Meara's return to England, which he thought disreputable—a letter addressed by him to the Admiralty, containing a charge against Sir Hudson Lowe which, if made at all, ought to have been made openly and substantiated by proof. This, therefore, must be set off against that appearance of credibility which is, as I think, distinguishable in O'Meara's book and in his conversation."

Lord Dudley's "impression" naturally counts for very little, but with regard to Sir George Cockburn two remarks may be made. First, Sir George Cockburn left St. Helena in June 1816, which was considerably more than a year before the Governor had a breach with O'Meara, so he could know nothing personally of the merits of the case; and, secondly, Lord Bathurst wrote to Sir Hudson Lowe in November 1818 that Sir G. Cockburn

was the first person who, on reading
the charges, declared that O'Meara ought
to be instantly dismissed the service.
Another statement (in the memoir of
O'Meara) is : "On his [O'Meara's] return
to England he was well received by the
Lords of the Admiralty, and is said to
have had the valuable post of surgeon to
Greenwich Hospital offered to him." Yes,
his "reception" consisted in his summary
dismissal from His Majesty's service—if
that is being "well received"—and the insinuation about Greenwich Hospital is
simply untrue. More than seventy years
ago Mr. Finlaison—O'Meara's old correspondent—wrote in a letter to the *Morning
Chronicle*:* "Mr. O'Meara having stated
in the latter part of his letter that I offered
him the lucrative situation of surgeon to
Greenwich Hospital, I beg leave to state,
in the most distinct manner, that I never

* Of March 3, 1823.

was authorised to make any such proposition, and that, therefore, it is but fair
to presume that I never could have done
so."

With regard to O'Meara's dismissal, the
defence is made that he could not have
brought the charge at the time, because Sir
Hudson Lowe would have seen it. But
surely he could have written it direct to
the Ministry, just as he wrote to Mr.
Finlaison without the knowledge of the
Governor, or again, as the Secretary to
the Admiralty reminded him, he could
have made the charge before the Admiral
on the station at St. Helena, who was
independent of the Governor. The defence
made is simply childish. We read again,
"The accuracy of O'Meara's narrative is
emphatically endorsed by Count Las
Cases." Very probably it is. Las Cases,
however, has quite enough to do to look
after his own character for "accuracy";

certainly he has not enough character for
two. This remark again is childish. In a
"note" the publishers state that advantage
has been taken of the narrative of Baron
Stürmer, and the *Life of Governor Lowe*
by Forsyth, to supplement "any important
passages or events by the impressions of
other observers at the moment—since
made accessible." Baron Stürmer was the
Austrian Commissioner resident at St.
Helena. He was, at the suggestion of the
British Government, removed from St.
Helena at the end of June 1818, in consequence of his persisting in unauthorised
communications with the French at Longwood; "but," adds Mr. Forsyth, "the un-
pleasantness of dismissal was veiled under
the guise of an appointment as Consul-
General for Austria to the United States
of America." He was hardly likely, therefore, to say much in favour of Sir Hudson
Lowe, though he was a frequent guest at

his table. It is true the new and anony-
mous editor does sometimes refer in a foot-
note in small print to Mr. Forsyth's book,
but in such a way as to leave the impression that O'Meara and Forsyth agree in substance but differ in some details. Forsyth,
as I need hardly remind the reader, is
flatly contradicting O'Meara nearly all
the time. Some of the most flagrant and
obvious misstatements of fact on the part
of O'Meara are omitted; for instance,
those contained in the entries of July 6,
1816, and December 18, 1817. The former
entry is thoroughly exposed in the *Quarterly
Review* article of October 1822, the latter
by Forsyth. Some of the language previously attributed to Lord Amherst, who
called in at St. Helena on his return from
China, is omitted, Lord Amherst having
taken the trouble to disavow it expressly.
With regard to omissions, the publishers
state that some " purely repetitory passages

have been omitted, also the story of the
early days of Napoleon's butler, Cipriani."
Under which heading do they class the
omissions above specified? There is also
an additional chapter professing to continue
the narrative to the death of Napoleon.
The writer faithfully imitates O'Meara in
his regard for accuracy. For instance, he
says that, in January 1820, Napoleon "on
several occasions breakfasted at the house
of Sir Wm. Doveton on the other side
of the island." Napoleon *once* only did
so, and this was on October 4, 1820.*
Forsyth gives a minute description of it,
as being a thing that only occurred *once*.
Again, a description is given of a visit of
Miss Susanna Johnson, "the young and
pretty daughter of Lady Lowe," who "ven-
tured to come alone to Longwood," and

* On this occasion the worthy knight described
Napoleon's appearance in a phrase more expressive
than elegant : " He looked," he said, " as fat and as
round as a China pig."

of her accidentally meeting the Emperor, who gave her a rose. For this Montholon is quoted as authority; but the writer should have seen the absurdity of it, and Miss Lowe, the half-sister of Miss Johnson, writes: "A pure invention; such a thing was impossible."

Such then is the value of the evidence of the French and of O'Meara. They spoke of each other, it is true, in terms the reverse of flattering, but their object was the same—to further the political plans of Napoleon. The French attacked Sir Hudson Lowe on political grounds, O'Meara attacked him mainly for personal reasons. What evidence is there on the other side? To begin with, the charges are obviously over-stated. If true, they prove too much. If true, it is hardly conceivable that the admirals on the station in succession—viz., Sir Pulteney Malcolm, Admiral Plampin, and Admiral Lambert, would not have interfered. They, at any rate, cannot have been terrorised by Sir Hudson Lowe. We find, however, that Sir Pulteney Malcolm, who was present at the last and stormiest interview between the Governor and Napoleon, gives the strongest testimony to the self-control of Sir Hudson Lowe, and this has the more weight in that the Governor and the Admiral were not on the most cordial terms. Moreover, the character of a man is judged most correctly by those among whom he spends his life, for no man can be always acting. It is not denied that Sir Hudson Lowe was personally popular with the inhabitants of St. Helena. They voted him an address when leaving, which contained much more than conventional expressions of regret at his departure, and some years later (in 1828) when, returning from Ceylon, he called in at St. Helena, he was fêted enthusiastically by the people,

who gratefully remembered the justice and
kindliness of his rule.

I will now take the direct evidence in
favour of Sir Hudson Lowe. First is that
of Lieutenant-Colonel Basil Jackson, whom
I have already had occasion to quote. He
was a gentleman universally respected, and
died only a few years ago at the patriarchal
age of ninety-four. He first became known
to Sir Hudson Lowe as serving on the
Staff in the Netherlands in 1814 and 1815,
and the impression which Sir Hudson Lowe
made upon him on first acquaintance has
already been given. The impression was
mutually favourable, for, on being nomin-
ated Governor of St. Helena, Sir H. Lowe
invited Lieutenant Jackson to accompany
him. His duty was to keep Longwood
House and its appurtenances in a habitable
state, with strict orders to neglect nothing
that could tend to promote the comfort of
Napoleon and the persons of his suite.

Probably Lieutenant Jackson was on more friendly terms with the French than any other Englishman, and so had exceptional opportunities of knowing their real sentiments. At a later period he was Lieutenant-Colonel of the Royal Staff Corps and Professor of Military Surveying at the East India College at Addiscombe. As Colonel Jackson uniformly speaks in favour of Sir Hudson Lowe, and as nothing whatever can be alleged against his character, an attempt has been made to detract from the weight of his testimony by the assertion that he was from early youth a *protégé* of Sir Hudson Lowe—an assertion which is perfectly untrue; and further, it has somehow got abroad that Sir Hudson Lowe's second son, the late Major-General Edward William Lowe, married a daughter of Colonel Jackson. This statement actually finds a place in the notice of Major-General Lowe in the *Dictionary of National*

Biography, but it is a pure fabrication, and has naturally caused much pain to the widow of General Lowe, who is still living. It is a matter of fact that Major-General Lowe never even met Miss Jackson. As already noticed, directly after Sir Hudson Lowe's death in January 1844, Colonel Jackson wrote "A Slight Tribute to the Memory of Sir Hudson Lowe," which appeared in the *United Service Magazine* for March of that year. In 1877 he wrote "Notes and Reminiscences of a Staff Officer, chiefly relating to the Waterloo Campaign and to St. Helena matters during the captivity of Napoleon," from which I have quoted under the title of *Waterloo and St. Helena*. It is an amusing and interesting book, but unfortunately was published only for private circulation, and is consequently little known to the public. As regards Sir H. Lowe, the tone of these reminiscences is the same as that of the article written thirty-three years earlier. I shall have to quote again from this small volume. Meantime I give his description of the Governor of St. Helena as he appeared in 1816: "He stood 5 ft. 7 in., spare in make, having good features, fair hair, and eyebrows overhanging his eyes; his look denoted penetration and firmness, his manner rather abrupt, his gait quick, his look and general demeanour indicative of energy and decision. He was warm and steady in his friendships, and popular both with the inhabitants of the isle and the troops." Another witness, still more independent if possible than Colonel Basil Jackson, inasmuch as he never saw Sir Hudson Lowe till they met at St. Helena, is Mr. Walter Henry, Assistant-Surgeon of the 66th Regiment, who arrived in July 1817 and remained till the end. He was present at the *post-mortem* examination of Napoleon and sailed to England with

the French. I have already quoted
from his book, *Events of a Military
Life*. He thus writes generally of the
Governor :

"The Governor appeared to be much occupied with the cares and duties of his important
and responsible office, and looked very like a
person who would not let his prisoner escape
if he could help it. From first impressions I
entertained an opinion of him far from favourable; if therefore, notwithstanding this prepos-
session, my testimony should incline to the
other side, I can truly state that the change took
place from the weight of evidence, and in consequence of what came under my own observation in St. Helena. Since that time he has
encountered a storm of obloquy and reproach
enough to bow any person to the earth; yet
I firmly believe that the talent he exerted in
unravelling the intricate plotting constantly
going on at Longwood, and the firmness in
tearing it to pieces, with the unceasing vigilance
he displayed in the discharge of his arduous
and invidious duties, made him more enemies
than any hastiness of temper, uncourteousness of demeanour, or severity in his measures,

of which the world was taught to believe him guilty." *

Mr. Henry's evidence is quite opposed to O'Meara's, although he was on very friendly terms with that individual until he lost his character. However, his experiences at St. Helena, being merely an episode in his life and adventures, cannot from the nature of the case be as much known as they would have been if separately published. The evidence of these two gentlemen alone is sufficient to overthrow the gigantic fabric of fraud and misrepresentation which has for so many years done duty with the world, and more especially with the British public, as the true history of Napoleon at St. Helena. I will, however, bring forward another witness. In 1876 the *St. James's Magazine* published a series of papers purporting to be written by one Stewart, a pretended con-

* Henry, ii. pp. 9, 10.

fidential servant of Napoleon. " They are a series of ridiculous falsehoods," says Colonel Jackson. The late Admiral Rous, who was on the station at St. Helena during part of this period, and to whom reference is made in these papers, wrote to Colonel Jackson as follows, under date July 22, 1876 : "The account of Napoleon at St. Helena is a tissue of falsehoods. . . . I do not believe either Lowe or Reade [Sir Thomas Reade] was capable of performing any act derogatory to the character of a gentleman. To the best of my knowledge, all reports of ill-treatment to Napoleon were systematic falsehoods, fabricated with a view of keeping alive a sympathy in Europe to enable his friends to succeed in obtaining a more agreeable exile."*

It now becomes my duty to deal with the specific charges, which I hope the reader may be disposed to regard *upon*

* *Waterloo and St. Helena*, pp. 117, 118.

their merits. But before coming to them
it may be as well to say a few words (1) on
the personal character of Sir H. Lowe,
and (2) on certain special difficulties with
which he had to contend. First then, I
will at once allow that Sir Hudson Lowe
was not a perfect character. He had his
failings, of course, like every one else. He
felt keenly, perhaps too keenly, the responsibility of his position. The peace of the
world, he was told, depended on the faithful execution of his trust. " There is only
one thing now to look after, and that rests
with you," was the refrain continually
dinned into his ears. He needed no arguments to convince him of the importance
of his charge, and was sometimes almost
pedantic in his adherence to the letter of
his instructions. He was constantly re-
ferring the most trivial matters to the home
authorities—even some matters of which
he, being on the spot, was a far more

Sir Hudson Lowe and Napoleon

competent judge than they could be. His
correspondence shows an almost nervous
anxiety to put things right. The determination of Napoleon to hold no personal
intercourse with the Governor caused
difficulties which might have been ex-
plained in a moment, but which, when set
forth in the diplomatic style affected by
Las Cases, Bertrand, or Montholon,
assumed formidable proportions. This is
a real defect. If the Governor had possessed a little more of the bluntness of Sir
George Cockburn he could not, it is true,
have satisfied Napoleon and his attendants
(no one could have done that), but he
would have spared himself a good deal of
worry. Again, he certainly showed a want
of tact in some of his dealings with Napoleon. When the Emperor persistently
refused to recognise the title of " General
Bonaparte," the only one by which the
British Government would allow him to be

addressed, it is hardly likely that he would have accepted an invitation to dinner from the Governor to " General Bonaparte." This invitation to meet the Countess of Loudon, though made with the best intentions, was clearly a mistake, and it is no wonder that Napoleon regarded it as an insult. Again, near the close of his life Napoleon presented to the officers of the 20th Regiment, to which his then medical attendant, Dr. Arnott, belonged, Coxe's *Life of Marlborough*, which had been given to him by the Hon. Robert Spencer. Unfortunately, the Imperial title was written inside the books. On this account, though Sir Hudson Lowe did not forbid the acceptance of the volumes, he certainly discouraged it, and they were not accepted. Upon this incident one must agree with the remarks of Mr. Forsyth : " I cannot help thinking that Napoleon's kindly-meant present might, under all the circumstances, have been accepted, notwithstanding the style of Emperor was inscribed in the volumes. He did not send them as coming from 'the Emperor,' nor write the objectionable title in them ; nor was there much likelihood of a British regiment being seduced from its allegiance by adding to its library a few books, the gift of Napoleon. It does not appear that he ever heard of the fate of his present ; but if he had there is no doubt that he would have felt what had happened as a deliberate insult."

There is also a consensus of opinion that the Governor's manner was abrupt and reserved, even in the judgment of those most favourably disposed towards him. His son says of him : " In speaking he was frequently embarrassed for words ; and in society alternated very much between extreme taciturnity and vehement animation of discourse. Even the greatest excitement, however, scarcely made his diction fluent."* This, however, is about all that can fairly be urged against Sir Hudson Lowe. And what does it amount to? Such slight matters as are only mentioned in a minute scrutiny of character.

Secondly, besides the difficulties inherent in his position, Sir Hudson Lowe had others which seem to have been added as a wanton aggravation. Three foreign Commissioners were sent to St. Helena by the Governments of France, Russia, and Austria (Prussia did not send one). They were, however, not merely useless but a great source of annoyance to the Governor. Ostensibly they helped to guard Napoleon, but as England had undertaken that duty and would naturally not be interfered with, they had nothing in the world to do except to pass their time, which they did partly by enjoying the hospitality of the Governor and partly by engaging in intrigues against

* *United Service Magazine*, June, 1844, p. 295.

the Governor's authority with the French attendants of the Emperor. They transmitted reports to their respective Governments, but as Napoleon would not receive them in their official capacity, and as Sir Hudson Lowe would not allow them to be presented as private individuals, they had not much of importance to transmit. Lord Bathurst urged Sir Hudson Lowe to encourage the Commissioners "to amuse themselves by going to the Cape by way of change of scene," and Napoleon himself exclaimed : "What folly it is to send those Commissioners out here without charge or responsibility! They will have nothing to do but to walk about the streets and creep up the rocks." Of the Austrian Commissioner, Baron Stürmer, and how his career was terminated, I have already spoken. Count Balmain, the representative of Russia, was recalled at the end of the three years for which he was appointed. Before he left

he married Miss Charlotte Johnson, Lady
Lowe's eldest daughter by her first husband.
The Marquis de Montchenu, the French
Commissioner, remained to the end and
was the least objectionable of the three.
He is described as "pompous and harm-
less." Colonel Jackson says he was fond
of going out to whist parties, but seldom
invited others to his own house. From
this circumstance he acquired the sobri-
quet of "le Marquis de Monter-chez-
nous."* Mr. Henry gives an amusing
account of how he attended the Marquis
during an illness, for which he thought
he had a right to expect some pecuniary
fee. But the excellent Marquis gave him
something much more valuable in the
shape of a note—of thanks, which is
printed in full as a model for future
Commissioners who may wish to pay
their doctors economically and yet hand-

* *Waterloo and St. Helena*, p. 91.

somely. "Who," he adds, "would ex-
change such a letter for a gold snuffbox?
I am quite certain that I never shall."
Incidentally Mr. Henry here testifies to
the Governor's kindness of heart. The
Marquis was recommended change of
air. "As soon as Sir Hudson Lowe
heard this he invited him to Plantation
House; and I rode there to see him two
or three times a week until his health
became perfectly re-established." Again,
Mr. O'Meara, the surgeon of Napoleon,
should have been put in precisely the
same position as the French attendants.
They were forbidden to send or receive
letters except such as were first seen by
the Governor. This order of the British
Government was peremptory. The same
restriction should have been placed upon
the surgeon. As it was, he could cor-
respond how and with whom he chose.
If this simple precaution had been

observed an infinity of mischief would have been prevented.

But the worst of all, and the thing which put so much power into the hands of O'Meara, was the conduct of the British Government, which, viewed in itself, was utterly undignified : viewed from Sir Hudson Lowe's standpoint, was unfair and treacherous. As I have said before, O'Meara carried on a regular correspondence with Mr. Finlaison of the Admiralty, and was encouraged by Cabinet Ministers to write copious letters of gossip about Napoleon for the amusement of themselves and the Prince Regent! It is true Sir Hudson was informed of this after it had gone on for a long time, but it utterly stultified the express instructions of the Government as to correspondence. Thus O'Meara was emboldened to defy the authority of Sir Hudson Lowe, and if it had not been for his own infatuation he might have

done so to the end.   Mr. Henry's remarks
on this are worth quoting.   He says :

"I have been informed since, on authority
which I cannot doubt, that Mr. O'Meara had a
friend in London, the private secretary of Lord
M[elvi]lle, who found it convenient to have a
correspondent in St. Helena, then a highly
interesting spot, who should give him all the
gossip of the island for the First Lord of the
Admiralty, to be sported in a higher circle afterwards for the Prince Regent's amusement.   The
patronage of Lord M. was thus secured ; and
Mr. O'Meara, confident on this backing, stood
out stiffly against Sir Hudson Lowe.   The latter
was quite ignorant of this intrigue against the
proper exercise of his authority ; and when he
discovered it afterwards he found it was a
delicate matter to meddle with, involving the
conduct of a Cabinet Minister, and affecting,
possibly, the harmony of the Ministry.   Even
after the development of the vile poisoning
charge against the Governor, the influence of
the First Lord was exerted to screen O'Meara,
but in vain ; for Lord Liverpool exclaimed, as
in another well-known instance of a very different description, "It is too bad !"*

* Henry, ii. p. 43.

Thus, while one Cabinet Minister was writing to Sir Hudson Lowe commending him for his vigilance, and urging particular care to prevent clandestine correspondence, another Cabinet Minister was doing all he could to undermine the Governor's authority by encouraging a clandestine correspondence! I do not think Mr. Forsyth has made enough of this. What Governor ever before had at the same time to fight against open foes and treacherous friends? Fortunately for others, especially for the British Government, O'Meara was the sort of man who, if given enough rope, would be sure to hang himself; and so it proved. The Government did not, therefore, reap the full consequences of their own folly. It is certainly no thanks to *them* that Napoleon did not effect his escape.

Sir Hudson Lowe was too loyal to make any formal complaint, but a consciousness of the unfair position in which

he was placed is evident in a memorial
to Lord Liverpool which he drew up in
1824. It is indeed incredible, as Sir
Hudson Lowe there remarks, that the
members of the Government who enjoyed
O'Meara's gossip intended in the first
instance that he should be the medium
of communication to them of important
state information. Yet O'Meara saw his
advantage and immediately seized it. He
delivered up to Sir Hudson Lowe a letter
written by Count Montholon (the celebrated " Remonstrance ") which had been
left in his room for the purpose of being
sent home to be published in the *Morning
Chronicle*, and of which he said to the
Governor that he intended to make no
other use than to take extracts from it
for a friend in the Admiralty. He also
exhibited a letter marked " secret and confidential," encouraging his correspondence,
but not communications of this kind. The

Governor then cautioned him upon his correspondence with any individual upon matters of so delicate a nature, and added that the Governor himself was the proper channel for communications to His Majesty's Ministers. The merit would not be less his, as any information he might give would be conveyed in his own name. In spite of this, however, O'Meara resolved on a continuance of his communications, and, in order to obtain a guarantee for them, boldly made known the injunctions that had been laid upon him by Sir Hudson Lowe, and his arguments for disobeying them, and actually transmitted at the same time a copy of the very letter he had delivered up to Sir Hudson Lowe! Two months later he sent a still fuller communication, repeated the injunctions of Sir Hudson Lowe, and resolved to bring the question to an issue, "as to the approbation or otherwise that might be bestowed upon the continuance of his opposition in so important a point to the officer under whose authority he was placed." The replies to that letter were decisive as to the nature of Sir Hudson Lowe's future relations, not only with O'Meara himself, but with Napoleon (who had the wires thus placed in his own hands), with his followers, with the foreign Commissioners, to whom their purport must have been secretly communicated, and in short with all descriptions of persons whom there was any object in letting into the secret. " Words cannot convey," continues the Governor, " in more precise terms the approbation bestowed on the conduct of the person written to. It is unnecessary to say that this unfortunate proceeding rendered tenfold more difficult the execution of Sir Hudson Lowe's duties at St. Helena, and made it almost impossible for him to come to any right understanding with the persons under his charge—secretly stripped him of one of the chief attributes of his authority, while leaving him still the responsible person for the mischief which might spring from such interference with it."

In considering the charges against Sir Hudson Lowe, a clear distinction must be drawn between the acts of the British Government, in carrying out which the Governor was acting officially, and the personal acts of Sir Hudson Lowe. The first thing is the climate of St. Helena itself. It is "common form" with many French writers to assume that one of the objects the British Government had in sending Napoleon there was that he might be "assassinated" by the climate, which (they professed to think) would kill him in a few years. I verily believe this is the only charge made on behalf of the Emperor in which Sir Hudson Lowe is not involved.

Not even *his* malignity could affect the climate of St. Helena. All medical testimony is distinctly opposed to the notion that St. Helena is unhealthy, the death-rate being remarkably low. " For a tropical climate, only fifteen degrees from the Line, St. Helena is certainly a healthy island," writes Mr. Henry, "if not the most healthy of this description in the world. During one period of twelve months, we did not lose one man by disease out of four hundred of the 66th quartered at Deadwood (the camp near Longwood)." But this point is hardly worth labouring, because Las Cases says in his journal that Napoleon remarked to him : "After all, as a place of exile, perhaps St. Helena was the best. In high latitudes we should have suffered greatly from cold, and in any other island of the tropics we should have expired miserably under the scorching rays of the sun. This rock is wild and barren no doubt ; the climate is monstrous and unwholesome ; but the temperature, it must be confessed, is mild." In accordance with the curious fatality that attends the charges brought in connexion with the exile of Napoleon, we have French evidence as to the desirability of St. Helena as a place in which to settle. In a report published in 1804 at Paris, *by order of the First Consul*, St. Helena was called a terrestrial paradise, where the air was pure and the sky serene, where health shone in every countenance, and diseases contracted in India were immediately cured. As to the death of Napoleon, all the doctors who attended the *post-mortem* examination certified that the disease of which the Emperor died was cancer of the stomach—a disease which, I need hardly say, is unaffected by climate. O'Meara was absolutely wrong in his diagnosis of "chronic hepatitis," and it is a very remarkable fact *that it was owing to the good condition of the liver that life was preserved so long.* "The liver acted as a kind of cork or stopper to the opening in the coat of the stomach formed by the ulcer, and prevented the escape of the contents of the stomach, which must have caused immediate death."*

If Napoleon was to be detained at St. Helena certain measures had to be taken to prevent his escape, and also to prevent communications with adherents in Europe or elsewhere, who might form conspiracies and raise revolutions. The instructions of the British Government to Sir Hudson Lowe are contained in a despatch of Sept. 12, 1815, of which it is necessary to quote only the following passage: "You will observe that the desire of His Majesty's Government is to allow every indulgence

* Forsyth, iii. 293, and Dr. Shortt's evidence there quoted.

to General Bonaparte which may be com-
patible with the entire security of his
person : that he should not by any means
escape, or hold communication with any
person whatever (excepting through your
agency), must be your unremitted care ;
and these points being made sure, every
resource and amusement which may serve
to reconcile Bonaparte to his confinement
may be permitted." Sir Hudson Lowe
considered these the two leading points of
his instructions—personal security and the
prevention of unauthorised communication. It is generally represented that the
restrictions imposed were unnecessarily
harsh, and that they were rendered much
more intolerable by the harshness and
brutality of the Governor in carrying them
out. An examination will show that as
regards the Governor the precise opposite
was the case. The harshness of the restrictions, such as it was, was much miti-

gated by the kindness and consideration of Sir Hudson Lowe, and the nearest approach to a rebuke that he ever received from the Government was owing to his not insisting sufficiently upon their instructions being obeyed. The Marquis de Montchenu, the French Commissioner, complained to his Government of the lenity of Sir Hudson Lowe,* and General Gourgaud said at St. Helena to the Russian Commissioner that if he had been in the Governor's situation he would have acted with more rigour. " I would have confined them more closely ; he [*i.e.*, Sir Hudson Lowe] has good right to complain [of the manner in which Napoleon conducted himself]."† In October 1820

* His despatches to the French Government are contained in the French archives and were there found by M. Georges Firmin Didot some years ago. Since then M. Didot has published the book mentioned in the Bibliography at the end of this volume.

† "Je les aurais bloqués plus étroitement : il a cause de se plaindre," Forsyth, ii. 190.

H.M.S. *Owen Glendower*, commanded by
the Hon. Robert Spencer, arrived at St.
Helena. Captain Spencer arrived pre-
possessed in Napoleon's favour and believing that he was harshly treated, but
before quitting the island he quite changed
his opinion and said to the Governor that
"if the precautions erred in any way, it
was more on the side of indulgence than
unnecessary restraint."

The principal specific instructions of the
Government were the following :—

(1) *That Napoleon was not to be allowed
the title of Emperor, but was always to be
styled General Bonaparte.* This was from
first to last a source of endless discomfort
and difficulty. Certainly the British
Government were quite justified in their
refusal to allow the title of Emperor
to one whom they had not recognised
as such in the height of his prosperity,
and Sir Walter Scott strenuously defends

them, but it is just because they had
refused the title to the Emperor *then*
that they could afford to be generous
now. I am, therefore, of the opinion of
Mr. Henry and Mr. Forsyth that it is
a point which might have been conceded
without loss of dignity. The latter observes : "It seemed puerile in us to
ignore a title by which he will be known
in history as certainly as Augustus or
Charlemagne. It cannot be urged that to
recognise Napoleon as Emperor would
have been to abandon the cause of the
Bourbons, for we had previously concluded
the treaty of Amiens with him as the *de
facto* ruler of France ; and we had no right
to impose either a king or a form of government upon that country." However this
may be, all the odium of insisting upon
this point fell upon Sir Hudson Lowe, who
had no choice in the matter. We cannot
be surprised that Napoleon himself and

his attendants always insisted upon the title of " Emperor," and Sir Hudson Lowe was often obliged to return letters and other documents to them in consequence. Soon after the arrival of Sir Hudson Lowe, all Napoleon's suite and servants had to sign a declaration of submission to the terms on which they were to be allowed to remain on the island, and the Government allowed them to refer to Napoleon as the " Emperor." In consequence of this all the declarations were sent back by Government and had to be signed over again without any mention of the obnoxious title. There was then some theatrical display, Napoleon's suite at first declaring that they would rather be sent away than submit to such a degradation, as they professed to consider it. However, when they found that Sir Hudson Lowe was not to be trifled with on this point they gave in, General Gourgaud setting the example, much to the relief of Napoleon.*

(2) *That no letters or packets were to be sent or received by the French unless they were first seen by Sir Hudson Lowe.* This restriction was most vexatious, and, after all, useless. Sir Walter Scott observes most truly that when this restriction was placed upon *all* communications any person would feel a certain amount of sympathy, and be disposed to aid the exiles by conveying letters, &c., while if they had been allowed to make use of the ordinary post it would have been found much more difficult to prevail on people to convey letters secretly. But the chief objection is the fatal one that the regulation could not possibly be thoroughly carried out, and we know that the French never had any difficulty in carrying on a correspondence with Europe. Countess Bertrand on the voyage home

* Forsyth, i. 327.

frankly stated this to Mr. Henry, and General Gourgaud before his departure said to Major Gorrequer, the Governor's Military Secretary, "I might if I wished have sent away every week a packet to England." Captain Ripley, of H.E.I.C. ship *Regent*, who landed at St. Helena in May 1819, stated that he was offered £600 if he would be the bearer of a letter from the French to Europe. But I need not multiply instances, as the fact is undisputed, and the French used to boast of it. In October 1817 Napoleon wrote some remarks upon a speech of Lord Bathurst which had been recently made in the House of Lords in answer to one of Lord Holland moving for documents to show the treatment of Napoleon at St. Helena. On this occasion Sir Hudson Lowe departed from his instructions and allowed a sealed packet to be sent to Lord Liverpool, although he knew (or rather *because* he knew) that it contained complaints against himself. The French, however, scarcely appreciated the delicacy of his conduct, for at the same time they sent clandestinely a copy of the " Remarks " to be published in England on arrival. " Thus," says Mr. Forsyth, " the poison of calumny was disseminated abroad long before Sir Hudson Lowe ever knew, much less could reply to, the charges that were brought against him." Napoleon, it is well known, had immense pecuniary resources in Europe, and it is quite possible that by a correspondence he might have caused another revolution. I cannot, therefore, quite agree with Sir Walter Scott that the object aimed at by preventing clandestine correspondence might have been secured in some other way. I see no way by which this object could absolutely have been attained. It was a risk that had to be run.

(3) *That Napoleon should be seen by the*

orderly officer twice within the twenty-four hours, and that after nightfall sentinels should be placed round the house. It is obvious that there was no duty more difficult to carry out than the instruction that Napoleon should be seen by the orderly officer, and yet none that was of more importance for the security of his person. Sir Walter Scott considers that if this order were strictly enforced nearly all the others might have been neglected. Napoleon and his attendants systematically threw every obstacle in the way of the unfortunate orderly officer, and Sir Hudson Lowe often had to be content with very indirect evidence of the presence of Napoleon at Longwood, and sometimes days passed without his being seen at all. In spite of the extra pay, no officer was willing to hold this position longer than he could help. As to one of them (Captain Blakeney), O'Meara in his long letter to the Admiralty stated that he had long been weary of a situation in which his "honourable feelings and sentiments were wounded by Sir Hudson Lowe's having required him to make a report of the conversation and action of the persons with whom he daily sat down to table in that confidence always existing amongst brother officers." This, however, is only one of O'Meara's misstatements. Captain Blakeney himself wrote to Count Bertrand and stigmatised a similar statement as "false" and an "infamous calumny," and said he resigned because his situation deprived him of the society of his brother officers. His brother officers of the 66th also signed a declaration that they had never heard Captain Blakeney make use of any of the expressions attributed to him, or any words to that effect. Very amusing accounts are given by Captain Nicholls, though not perhaps so amusing to him, of the shifts to which he was put to carry out this irksome duty. He mentions being on his feet as much as ten hours at a time in order to get a glimpse of the Emperor. He says, for instance, one day that he caught a sight of him while he was strapping his razor. On another he saw the top of a cocked hat moving about which he presumed to be Napoleon's. Once, when he applied to Count Montholon for help, the Count suggested that he could see him through the keyhole! At length Lord Bathurst lost patience, and wrote that if Napoleon's system of seclusion continued, Sir Hudson Lowe must "adopt some compulsory mode of learning a fact indispensable to the prevention of his escape." It is one thing to write despatches from Downing Street and another to carry them out at St. Helena, and in spite of all the trouble that was given on this point, Sir Hudson Lowe never did have recourse to any compulsory measure. As to the post-

ing of sentinels after sunset, Lord Bathurst
made an effective answer to Lord Holland's
complaint on that head. He said in his
speech :

> "Sentinels were stationed there after sunset,
> and Napoleon had expressed his dislike to walk
> when he was thus watched. Sir H. Lowe, with
> every desire to attend to his wishes, after that
> fixed the sentinels in places where they would
> not look on him. Would their Lordships wish
> these sentinels to be removed altogether, just at
> the time when it was most likely that he should
> escape? Let them suppose for a moment that,
> instead of debating on the motion of the noble
> Lord, intelligence was brought them by Sir
> Hudson Lowe that General Bonaparte had
> actually escaped. Let them suppose that,
> instead of sitting to discuss whether a little
> more or little less restriction should be imposed,
> they had thus to examine Sir Hudson Lowe at
> their bar. How and when did he escape?—In
> the early part of the evening, and from his
> garden. Had his garden no sentinels?—The
> sentinels were removed. Why were they re-
> moved?—General Bonaparte desired it—they
> were hurtful to his feelings; they were then
> removed, and thus was he enabled to escape.

What would their Lordships think of such an
answer? He begged them to consider the
situation of Sir Hudson Lowe, in what a painful
and invidious station he was placed. If General
Bonaparte escaped, the character and fortune of
Sir Hudson Lowe were ruined for ever; and if
no attempts were made to effect that escape,
there would not be wanting some, from false
motives of compassion, to reproach him for
those restrictions which had probably prevented
those attempts from being made."

(4) *That the best house on the island
should be assigned to Napoleon, with the
exception of Plantation House, the country
residence of the Governor.* I admit at
once that it would have been better
if Plantation House had been given up
to Napoleon, but the orders of Government were positive, and Sir Hudson Lowe
had to carry them out. Longwood was
the next best house, the residence of the
Lieutenant-Governor. Napoleon had himself selected it when riding with Sir George

* Speech in the House of Lords, March 18, 1817.

Cockburn, soon after his arrival in the
island. Materials were sent out from
England for the purpose of constructing a
new house. When the materials came to
hand, Sir Hudson Lowe wrote to Napoleon
asking whether he would like to have a new
house erected, or additions made to the old
one. Receiving no answer, the Governor
went personally to wait upon the Emperor
and obtain his decision. The only answer
he could get was that the Emperor would
prefer a new house, but that it would take
five or six years to build, and he knew he
would not be so long on the island. Sir
Hudson Lowe then proceeded to make
alterations in the old house, but Napoleon
disapproved of this, though it was done for
the purpose of lodging his attendants.
One cannot object, of course, to Napoleon's
having a choice either of the new house or
the old one, or between alterations and no
alterations, but the objection is that he

made every attempt to improve his residence the foundation of a charge against Sir Hudson Lowe, and that he watched the moment when attention was being paid to his wishes to make that attention a source of complaint. For the summer of 1817, with a view to secure Napoleon's comfort, Sir Hudson Lowe applied to Miss Mason, a lady who lived at a house called Pleasant Mount, which had shady trees and water. She was willing to let it for £100 a month, and Sir Hudson Lowe at once wrote to Count Bertrand stating the advantages of the situation, and telling him that if Napoleon would accept the house it was at his disposal for the summer months. *To this letter no answer was ever returned.* At length, when it was obvious that there was no prospect of his recall, Napoleon did condescend to examine plans for a new house, which was actually completed a short time before his death, though, in consequence of his illness, never occupied by him. There was an iron railing some distance from the house, of the simple kind that is often put up before houses in England. It could not be seen from the house, but Napoleon took a dislike to it and said it formed an "iron cage." Sir Hudson Lowe immediately ordered it to be discontinued, and, subsequently ascertaining that the objection was not so much against the railing itself as against its too great proximity to the house, he had it placed further back. Near the end of his life Napoleon conveyed to Sir Hudson Lowe through Count Montholon his thanks to the British Government for having caused such a house to be built for him and to Sir Hudson Lowe himself for the pains he had taken in its construction.

(5) *That certain limits should be as-signed within which Napoleon should be*

at liberty to walk or ride unattended.
Under Sir George Cockburn a circuit of
twelve miles was allowed within which
Napoleon might walk or ride unattended,
while he might go anywhere on the island
attended by a British officer. Surely the
limit of twelve miles was ample. It is
true that for a time Sir Hudson Lowe
made some modification in this arrange-
ment, but as this is a matter rather
personal to the Governor than connected
with his instructions from home, I will deal
with it later. The limits to be fixed were
left to the Governor, the Government only
stipulating that there should be some limits,
and that these should be reasonable.

These were the principal instructions of
the British Government. With regard to
the first three, Sir Hudson Lowe actually
relaxed them, and had to defend his
conduct to the home authorities for so
doing. As to the fourth, Napoleon at last

Sir Hudson Lowe and Napoleon

admitted the pains which the Governor took to consult his comfort. The fifth I postpone for the moment. And yet all these relaxations were represented by the French as "caprice"!

On this point Sir Hudson Lowe writes, not without dignity and pathos: "When you have found me accused of some atrocious cruelty, harshness, or injustice, be assured such has not merely not been committed, but that it is more than probable I have been guilty of some act of indulgence or attention on the very occasion diametrically opposite to that of which I have been accused."*

I will now come to the charges against Sir Hudson Lowe not so immediately connected with his instructions, and of a personal rather than official nature. None of them present any difficulty.

(1) *That Napoleon was on comparatively*

* From an unpublished letter.

*good terms with Sir George Cockburn, and
that therefore it must have been the fault
of Sir Hudson Lowe that Napoleon took
such a vehement dislike to him.* After
the Admiral left this was constantly said
by Napoleon and his attendants, but as
long as he was acting Governor Napoleon
could hardly say anything bad enough
about him. I have already quoted the
language in which he anticipated the
arrival of Sir Hudson Lowe. When the
Admiral refused to forward sealed packets
to England, Napoleon burst out: "Who is
the Admiral? I never heard his name
mentioned as conquering in a battle, either
singly or in general action. 'Tis true he
has rendered his name infamous in America,
which I heard of, and he will now render it
so here on this detestable rock. I believe,
however, that he is a good sailor. Next
to your Government exiling me here the
worst thing they could have done, and the

most insufferable to my feelings, is sending me with such a man as *him!*" * At another time he is represented as saying: " In fact, I expect nothing less from your Government than that they will send out an executioner to despatch me. They send me here to a horrible rock, where even the water is not good; they send out a *sailor* with me who does not know how to treat a man like me, and who puts a *camp* under my nose, so that I cannot put my head out without seeing my jailors. Here we are treated like felons; a proclamation issued for nobody to come near or touch us, as if we were so many lepers or had the itch!" † Napoleon's feeling against the Admiral is also shown by the fact that he attributed the choice of an unusually early hour for the first interview with Sir Hudson Lowe to a desire on Sir George Cockburn's

* From a letter of O'Meara to Mr. Finlaison, dated March 16, 1816, given by Forsyth, i. pp. 66 foll.
† *Ibid.*

part to embroil him with the new Governor.
It was plainly the object of Napoleon and
his suite to play off Sir Hudson Lowe
against Sir George Cockburn, and when
the latter had gone, then Sir George Cockburn against Sir Hudson Lowe.

(2) *That Sir Hudson Lowe innovated
upon the arrangements made by Sir
George Cockburn and frequently even
changed his own regulations.* This is
what has caused Sir Walter Scott, writing
on imperfect information, to speak of the
Governor's "want of steadiness of purpose," and if it were really the case that
the Governor *did* frequently alter his
regulations he would certainly have shown
himself to be an unfit person for the important post he occupied. But what are
the facts? As we have seen, the original
limits within which Napoleon could walk
or ride unattended embraced a circuit of
twelve miles. In October 1816 Sir
Hudson Lowe cut off from it a ravine

where were some cottages. This also cut off a road on the other side of the ravine. As, however, Napoleon complained bitterly of not being allowed to ride along a road which, when it was open to him, he had never once made use of, Sir Hudson soon withdrew the regulation and restored the road to the limits. Every subsequent change, as Mr. Forsyth shows, was in Napoleon's favour, and more and more space was afterwards accorded to him, until even Montholon warmly thanked Sir Hudson Lowe for what he had done for them. All that is required to vindicate Sir Hudson Lowe from the charge of vacillation in this matter is to state the facts. On two other points it cannot be denied that there had been a certain amount of laxity on the part of Sir George Cockburn, and Sir Hudson Lowe had to insist on a stricter carrying out of Government's instructions. Sir George Cockburn was only in charge from October 1815 to April 1816, and himself admitted that if he had been staying longer he should have drawn the reins a little tighter, inasmuch as he saw some of the evils that were accruing. In Sir George Cockburn's time the sentinels were drawn round the house at nine o'clock. Now, as there was (on an average) an interval of three hours between sunset and nine o'clock, and as this interval gave an opportunity for eluding the vigilance of the guards, Sir Hudson Lowe had the sentinels posted at sunset; but, with that deference to the susceptibilities of Napoleon which he always manifested, the sentinels were drawn only round the garden at sunset, and not round the house till nine. Again, it had been permitted by Sir George Cockburn that passes signed by Bertrand only should give access to Longwood, and also an invitation to dinner sent by Count

Bertrand to any person who had been presented to Napoleon should be received by the guard as a pass. It was obvious that this permission was liable to abuse, and that under cover of it sealed communications might pass. And so it proved, for Count Bertrand soon asserted that Sir George Cockburn had authorised a sealed correspondence. Sir George Cockburn himself told Sir Hudson Lowe that if he had foreseen that Count Bertrand's house at Longwood would have been so long in construction (he lived at first at Hutt's Gate, about two miles from Longwood) he would not have given this latitude. These are all the changes that were made by Sir Hudson Lowe, and it will be seen that they were made partly in order to comply more strictly with definite instructions, partly to mitigate, as far as he could, the inconvenience of the situation of the exiles.

(3) *That Sir Hudson Lowe was harsh*

in temper and coarse in language. These
charges are made against the Governor,
especially as regards his interviews with
Napoleon. From what has been written
on this subject it might be thought that
Sir Hudson Lowe was in the habit of
riding to Longwood once or twice a week
for the purpose of abusing and maltreating
the captive Emperor. But, as already
remarked, there were only five interviews
between them altogether, and it was only
at the last three that any stormy scenes
occurred. The third interview was mostly
taken up by Napoleon with abuse of Sir
Hudson Lowe, and he admitted afterwards
to Las Cases: "I behaved very ill to him
no doubt. However, the Governor proved
himself very insensible to my severity; his
delicacy did not seem wounded by it. I
should have liked to have seen him evince
a little anger or pull the door violently
after him when he went away." In other

words, as Mr. Forsyth puts it, the Governor
behaved with dignity and forbearance during
this explosion of bad temper on the part of
Napoleon. The fourth interview was much
of the same nature as the third, Napoleon
spending most of it in abuse; but the
fifth and last, on August 18, 1816, was
the most violent exhibition of Napoleon's
manners. He positively exhausted the
vocabulary of insult and vituperation. At
this interview Admiral Sir Pulteney Malcolm was present, and the Emperor had
recourse to the peculiarly irritating trick
of abusing a man in his presence but in
language addressed to a third person, for
nearly all of what he said was to the
Admiral. It was at this interview that he
called Sir Hudson a *sbirro Siciliano* (a
Sicilian thieftaker). Napoleon himself
afterwards admitted that his own conduct
had been as offensive as possible, and did
the justice to acknowledge that Sir Hudson

Lowe had never shown him any want of respect, that the only thing noticeable was the abrupt way in which he had retired, while the Admiral withdrew with numerous salutations. And this is all, that after being subjected to a torrent of unmerited abuse Sir Hudson Lowe withdrew without a bow! The coolness with which Sir Hudson Lowe bore his insults increased Napoleon's anger, for he said: "This is the second time in my life that I have spoilt my affairs with the English. Their phlegm leads me on and I say more than I ought."* It was at this interview that the Governor is said to have laid his hand on his sword—a fable which not only Sir Hudson Lowe indignantly denied, but of which O'Meara also says that he knew it to be incorrect. The real grievance of Napoleon was clearly that he could not make the Governor lose command of

---

* "Leur flegme me laisse aller." Forsyth, i. 256.

his temper, that his demeanour was imperturbable. It is perfectly true that, as Lord Bathurst reminded Sir Hudson Lowe, no language of Napoleon, in the situation in which he was, could be regarded as an insult; but, however much that may be the case, things can be said which it requires extraordinary self-control not to resent. Napoleon was of course fully aware of this, and used his privilege to the full. On the evening of that day Lieutenant Jackson was dining with the Admiral, who spoke freely of the interview, and bore willing testimony to the cool replies and admirable forbearance of Sir Hudson Lowe.* It is admitted by his son that Sir Hudson Lowe's temper was *naturally* "violent and hasty enough"†—all the greater credit to him then for his admirable self-

---

* From a letter of Colonel Jackson to Mr. Henry, see Henry, ii. 58.

† "Memoir," *United Service Magazine*, June 1844.

control. It is right to state that in an
unpublished memorandum made long after,
Sir Hudson Lowe writes : " It is but justice
to Napoleon to observe that he was never
so very coarse and rude in his manner or
language as he has been represented to
have been : many a lie has thus been
fathered upon him." Finally, to dispose
of these charges, I will quote from a letter
of Colonel Jackson to Mr. Henry, provoked
by Mr. Henry's having, in his first edition,
made some remark about Sir Hudson
Lowe's temper on the authority of O'Meara,
which in the second edition he withdrew
on ascertaining that O'Meara's statement
was unworthy of credit, while at the
same time he says for himself that, during
four years' acquaintance with Sir Hudson
Lowe, "the demeanour of this much-
injured man was always gentlemanly and
courteous, both to myself and all around
him." Colonel Jackson writes as follows :

Sir Hudson Lowe and Napoleon

"Few persons, if any, are better acquainted with Sir Hudson Lowe than myself. When he was Quartermaster-General in 1814 and 1815, I was Deputy Assistant in the Department and attached to the office, when I was with him every day, and had indeed more communication with him than others, and sometimes of a confidential character. I also at that time saw him when certain circumstances gave him much annoyance; but cannot recollect any single instance of his breaking out into any unseemly bursts of anger, or showing real uncourteousness. He was very much liked by all who served under him, being at all times kind, considerate, generous, and hospitable. . . Depend upon it the reports spread of Sir Hudson Lowe's 'bursts of un-dignified and reprehensible passion' were wholly without foundation as regards the persons at Longwood, and most grossly exaggerated as regards ourselves. I have heard Sir George Bingham speak highly of Sir Hudson; your friend, General Nicol, does the same, and, in fact, most of the officers of rank who were at St. Helena, and I cannot remember to have heard any one complain of Sir Hudson's temper. Like other men, he is liable to the infirmities of our nature; but want of proper self-command has never been one of his defects."

At St. Helena

Even Sir Walter Scott (in his *Life of Napoleon*), whom no one would ever accuse of unwillingness to do justice to the reputation of another, or suspect of unfairness in the use of materials placed at his command, considers that Sir Hudson Lowe failed in " proper command of temper in his intercourse with Napoleon," and in " steadiness of purpose." On the second point I have already said enough. As to the charge against Sir Hudson Lowe's temper, we must remember that Sir Walter had not the materials for a complete defence. This required an inspection of the minutes made by Major Gorrequer of the conversations held, a comparison of O'Meara's printed narrative with his private letters, and the consideration of many documents in Sir Hudson Lowe's possession which Sir Walter Scott had no opportunity of perusing. Moreover, at the time he wrote, Sir Hudson Lowe was in Ceylon, so he could

not consult him personally. It is however
impossible to suppose that Sir Walter can
have attentively read the correspondence
between Lord Bathurst and the Governor
of St. Helena, and the other official documents, and weighed their evidence against
that of such authors as O'Meara, Las Cases,
and Antommarchi. In them there is not
a line to warrant the conclusion that Sir
Hudson Lowe ever regarded Napoleon as
"an object of resentment, and open to
retort and retaliation." Sir Archibald
Alison's language (in his *History of Europe*)
is more unfavourable. He says : "Sir
Hudson Lowe, who was appointed to the
military command of the island, proved an
unhappy selection. His manner was rigid
and unaccommodating, and his temper of
mind was not such as to soften the distress
which the Emperor endured during his
detention." Lord Campbell is still more
condemnatory in his " Life of Lord Eldon "

(*Lives of the Chancellors*). He says: "As
things were managed, I am afraid it will
be said that he (Napoleon) was treated, in
the nineteenth century, with the same cruel
spirit as the Maid of Orleans was in the
fifteenth ; and there may be tragedies on
the Death of Napoleon, in which Sir
Hudson Lowe will be the *sbirro*, and
even Lord Eldon may be introduced as the
stern old councillor who decreed the hero's
imprisonment." But these writers had no
more means of knowing the truth than
what Sir Walter Scott possessed, and it is
"impossible not to see that they have all
been influenced in their opinions by the
assertions of authors, the bitterest enemies
of Sir Hudson Lowe, who had hitherto
occupied the field of narrative with regard
to the events at St. Helena."* As I have
already remarked, all this has been altered
since the publication of Mr. Forsyth's book,

* Forsyth, i. 125.

and those who now believe that Sir Hudson
Lowe was guilty of harshness of temper
and coarseness of language will believe
almost anything.

(4) *That Sir Hudson Lowe gradually procured the dismissal of the faithful attendants
of Napoleon with the intention of aggra-
vating the prisoner's painful situation and
getting him more and more into his power.*
Las Cases, Gourgaud, Bertrand and Montholon were the four principal sharers of
Napoleon's exile, and they, together with
the surgeon O'Meara, were those most
about his person. The circumstances
attending the removal of O'Meara have
already been narrated, and it has been
shown that Sir Hudson Lowe would have
endeavoured to procure his removal at an
earlier period, had it not been that he was
unwilling to remove one to whom the
Emperor seemed attached. At the close
of 1816 Las Cases was sent away owing

to the discovery of unauthorised communications by him. I need not go into the
details, as they are not in dispute. A
servant of Las Cases who was going to
Europe was accidentally discovered to have
a letter concealed in the lining of his waist-
coat. But it is very doubtful whether Las
Cases, in spite of his protestations, had any
objection to leave Longwood. He had to
sail first to the Cape of Good Hope, in
accordance with the instructions from
England that those who left St. Helena
should go first to the Cape, and, in the
interval before a ship was ready for him,
Sir Hudson Lowe gave him the option of
returning to Longwood, but he never
availed himself of it. O'Meara says, in a
letter to Mr. Finlaison, that in his opinion
Las Cases had planned the whole scheme
on purpose to be detected, being heartily
tired of his residence in the island ; in other
words, that (in sporting language) "he

was riding for a fall." I do not think the evidence goes as far as this, but it is hardly uncharitable to suppose with Colonel Jackson that he was " very glad to get out of the mess," * in spite of the fact that he was genuinely attached to his master. Sir Hudson Lowe gave him a friendly letter of introduction to Lord Charles Somerset, Governor of the Cape of Good Hope, who thus wrote back some time afterwards, when Las Cases' *Journal* had been published : " The whole of the Count's publication (if it really be his) is so contemptible a performance that I own his wailings and his complaints, as far as they involve myself, are matters perfectly indifferent to me ; with regard to his assertions respecting the Cape and his treatment here, I know them to be so absolutely and impudently false that it is not too much to presume that there is

* Henry, ii. 47.

not a single correct statement in the whole book." *

In the beginning of 1818 General Gourgaud of his own accord applied for leave to return to Europe, which was granted. For a long time Napoleon had ceased to be cordial to him. He was hardly on speaking terms with Bertrand, and at open enmity with Montholon. "I used," says Colonel Jackson, "frequently to call and chat with him, when he would often lament his hard fate, and sigh for *La belle France*, for Paris and *les Boulevards*. At length *maladie de pays* got the better of him, and he determined to leave Longwood. Sir Hudson Lowe sent for me, and, having mentioned Gourgaud's wish, asked whether it would be agreeable for me to reside with him until an opportunity should offer for his quitting St. Helena. . . . . Accordingly, General Gourgaud and myself were in-

* Forsyth, iii. 148.

stalled in a comfortable house, in which
servants and a table were provided for us
at the expense of Government. We lived
near the residence of the Austrian and
Russian Commissioners, whom we occasionally visited, and nothing could exceed
the attention and hospitality of Sir Hudson
Lowe to General Gourgaud." * Colonel
Jackson then gives a remarkable instance
of the Governor's generosity :

"In justice to that excellent and grossly
maligned individual, Sir Hudson Lowe, I shall
now relate a circumstance which I am sure
General Gourgaud will be ready to confirm.
When the latter removed from Longwood, I
accompanied him to the Governor's residence,
when I took an opportunity to leave him and
Sir Hudson *tête-à-tête*. Immediately on our
riding from Plantation House together, the
General broke out into strong exclamations of
surprise that Sir Hudson should simply have
received his visit as the call of one gentleman
upon another, without ever alluding to Longwood during their conversation. 'I expected,

* Henry, ii. 48.

added he, ' that the Governor would have seized with avidity so favourable an occasion as my excited state offered to gather from me some information about the goings on at Longwood. *Je ne reviens pas de mon étonnement, non, je n'en reviens pas.* These expressions of surprise he repeated over and over again during our short ride.* I may add that I had many opportunities of remarking the really chivalrous delicacy of Sir Hudson in reference to General Gourgaud.

" Although the Emperor and the General did not part the best friends, yet, as it was known at Longwood that the latter was unprovided with funds, a considerable sum was offered to him by Napoleon, and even pressed on his acceptance when leaving Longwood, which he declined to receive. But soon after, when about to embark for England, the poor General found the usual inconveniences of a penniless position, and sent me to Longwood to ask Marshal Bertrand for a loan of two or three hundred pounds. The Marshal declined, saying that the Emperor had offered him a much larger sum, the refusal of which was most disrespectful ; but added that

---

* The forbearance of Sir Hudson Lowe in not questioning General Gourgaud is nothing remarkable. What is more noticeable is the General's surprise at it.

even then, if General Gourgaud would accept
the Emperor's gift, he would also lend him the
sum he asked.

"Gourgaud was a good deal distressed by the
refusal of Bertrand, which was quite unexpected,
but still declined placing himself under a pecuniary obligation to Napoleon; and would have
sailed to England without a shilling but for Sir
Hudson Lowe, who, as soon as he learned the
circumstances, sent him by note an order for one
hundred pounds on his bankers in London."*

To this letter of Colonel Jackson, Mr.
Henry adds: "The honourable traits he
gives of Sir Hudson Lowe are in my humble
opinion quite in keeping with the true
character of that distinguished officer."

Colonel Jackson tells us also that after
General Gourgaud's arrival in England he
was turned round again by politicians there
in favour of Napoleon, who told him that
otherwise he would be of no account. "This
he did by inditing a letter to Marie Louise
in which he inveighed against the treatment

* Henry, ii. 48-50.

of Napoleon at the hands of Government and Sir Hudson Lowe, which being duly published, Gourgaud fell to zero in the opinion of all right-minded persons."* We have seen in Mr. Henry's narrative how an attempt was made to bribe him to become *l'homme de l'Empereur.* After the departure of O'Meara, in July 1818, Mr. Stokoe, the surgeon of H.M.S. *Conqueror*, was, at the request of the Longwood people, appointed medical attendant to Napoleon; but as he was known to be a man of good nature and easy disposition he was strictly charged by the Governor and the Admiral to sign no document whatever without their knowledge and permission. "The new medical attendant," says Mr. Henry, "like many others, lost his wits in the presence of Napoleon, totally forgot his orders, and signed the first paper that was offered, for which disobedience the

* *Waterloo and St. Helena,* p. 103.

Admiral sent him home under arrest."
He was afterwards sent back to St.
Helena, tried by court-martial, and sen-
tenced to be dismissed the service, though
allowed a pension on account of his long
services. Of course the Stokoe affair has
been made a charge against Sir Hudson
Lowe. Next Dr. Verling, of the Royal
Artillery, was ordered to take up his abode
at Longwood, and after a short time he
was offered a very large bribe by Montholon if he would abandon the Governor
and attach himself to the Emperor, as
O'Meara had done. But Dr. Verling was
a man of a different stamp from poor
Stokoe. The Count's proposition was
indignantly rejected : the doctor mounted
his horse and rode to Plantation House,
reported the affair to the Governor, and
requested to be relieved from a post where
he was liable to such an insult. He could
not be relieved at the time, and remained

at Longwood until the arrival of Dr. Antommarchi. So much then for the "removal" of Las Cases, Gourgaud, and Stokoe. Count Bertrand and Montholon remained to the end, and were, as we have seen, on good terms with Sir Hudson Lowe after the death of Napoleon. Bertrand afterwards was so far from supporting the credit of O'Meara's book that he published in the *Constitutionnel* a letter, in which he stated it as due to the memory of Napoleon, to France and to Europe, to declare himself an utter stranger to the conversations reported in *A Voice from St. Helena.**

(5) *That enough money was not allowed for the support in proper style of Napoleon and his suite, and that in consequence some of Napoleon's plate had to be broken up and sold to supply the deficiency.* If we believe Las Cases, they were in actual

* *United Service Magazine,* June 1844, p. 293.

want of food; if we believe Napoleon himself, "there had been enough to eat supplied, though not enough to keep a proper table"; but if we look to the evidence of facts we can believe neither of them. The orders of Government were that the table was to be supplied on the scale of a general of the first rank. Sir Hudson Lowe, finding on his arrival that the amount of £8000 a year allowed by Government for the Longwood establishment was not sufficient, immediately, and on his own responsibility, raised it to £12,000 a year, which, if expenses had been kept within reasonable limits, would have been ample. Anything beyond this was defrayed by Napoleon himself. Personally the Emperor was not extravagant in his living, but the extravagance of his followers knew no bounds. In one of O'Meara's letters to Mr. Finlaison—the statement will be sought in vain in his book—he calls them "except one or two, the greatest gluttons and epicures he ever saw," and he goes on to describe their style of living. Each upper domestic was allowed a bottle of claret a day at the price of £6 per dozen, and the amount of wine consumed averaged two bottles a day per head for the whole establishment. The food was plentiful, but the quality sometimes left something to be desired. Colonel Jackson says, "provisions may not have been of the highest quality, though the best the island afforded."* That of course is the point, and Mr. Henry humorously complains of the inferior living that the 66th Regiment had to put up with. "The superior quality," he says, "of everything used at Longwood at this time was notorious. The purveyor for that establishment found means always to monopolise the best meat; his daily cart conveying

* *Waterloo and St. Helena*, p. 111.

provisions to Longwood often underwent the envious scrutiny of our officers, as they met it in the course of their rides, when the peevish exclamation, 'We can't get anything like that for the mess,' was generally the result."* We also find Dr. Baxter, the Deputy-Inspector of Hospitals at St. Helena, requesting the Governor to interfere "in the universal and sweeping monopoly of the contractors for Longwood," and complaining that he cannot get enough milk for the sick of the 53rd Regiment. On one occasion a complaint was made that not enough coals and wood was allowed. The Governor immediately ordered the allowance of coal to be doubled, the wood to remain the same, on account of the great scarcity of wood in the island. The next time they were out of wood the French servants broke up a bedstead and some shelves for the fires at Longwood,

* Henry, ii. 54, note.

pretending that they would not be allowed more wood. Napoleon approved of wood not being asked for, saying he could pay for it himself. The Governor remarked, on hearing of it, that this was always the way: they never would tell what they required, and then complained of the want of it. As to breaking up the plate, it was well known that Napoleon had plenty of ready money at his command, and that consequently this pretended sacrifice was made for the edification of the European public. O'Meara in a letter to Mr. Finlaison says of Napoleon, " In this he has also a wish to excite an odium against the Governor by saying that he has been obliged to sell his plate in order to provide against starvation, *as he himself told me was his object.*" Of a second sale of plate Montholon writes, " I was to persist in saying that his (Napoleon's) plate was his only resource at St. Helena ; and I received the order to have all the plate broken up, with the exception of twelve covers," thus admitting in so many words that the scheme was one to impose on the public. But the pretence of ill-treatment was not always consistently kept up, and we find towards the end of the time various acknowledgments by Montholon of the trouble which was taken to supply them properly. Thus, in January 1820, he said to Major Gorrequer, in reply to a question on the subject of provisions, "We can only congratulate ourselves on the manner in which we are served."

(6) *That Napoleon was not allowed to have a regular supply of books and newspapers, and that what were sent were often detained altogether, or for some time, by Sir Hudson Lowe.* This has been an effective charge, and, if there is any gradation in falsehood, one of the falsest. As for books, one work by Mr. Hobhouse (afterwards Lord Broughton), sent by the author to

Napoleon, was, it is true, detained by the Governor, because in one volume was written " Imperatori Napoleon." It may have been good or bad judgment to detain the volumes, but the point is that in a note to Sir Hudson Lowe Mr. Hobhouse expressly authorised detention of them, "if it be thought improper to give them at all to the person for whom they are destined." This seems to be the only case in which a book was kept back. On the other hand, many hundreds of pounds' worth of books were sent by booksellers to Napoleon and received by him. With regard to newspapers, Count Montholon writes in his " Remonstrance," which was meant for European consumption only : "We are prohibited from receiving the *Morning Chronicle*, the *Morning Post*, or any French papers ; occasionally a few odd numbers of the *Times* are sent to Longwood." To this the Governor replied, speaking in the third person : "General Bonaparte once sent a message to him requesting him to send him the *Morning Chronicle*, and he immediately sent the whole of those which he had then in his possession. No application was ever made to him to subscribe either to the *Morning Chronicle* or the *Morning Post*, or to any French journals. Had such an application been made he would have made the application known to his Government. It has not been odd numbers of the *Times* newspaper, but regular series of them, which have been constantly sent, the Governor never having kept back a single number. If any numbers were kept back it must have been done by his (Napoleon's) own followers, to whom they were always enclosed for him." O'Meara too says, in his *A Voice from St. Helena*, that very few newspapers were received, that "none except some unconnected numbers of the *Times, Courier,*

Observer, &c., with a few straggling French papers of a very old date, reached Longwood during his residence there, except in one instance, when he was permitted to take the *Morning Chronicle* for some weeks as a great favour, which was not again repeated."* And yet O'Meara had written to Sir Hudson Lowe on the previous June 20, in reply to inquiries of the Governor "to be informed of the names of such newspapers as General Bonaparte may have received." After giving the names of a good many English newspapers, he says: " *These, with the usual series of papers sent by yourself*, some French papers, and *Morning Chronicle* for October, November, and part of December, also sent by yourself, form the whole of the newspapers he has received." The truthful doctor thus disposes of himself. Yet this entry of March 28, 1818, is retained in the 1888 edition!

* *A Voice from St. Helena*, ii. 397, under March 28, 1818.

Sir Hudson Lowe and Napoleon

(7) *That Sir Hudson Lowe offered inducements to O'Meara to act as a spy, and on his refusal tried to ruin him.* This charge has been already dealt with by anticipation under the general account of O'Meara. We have also seen that the Governor abstained from putting questions to General Gourgaud about Longwood at a time when he might have obtained much information. I will add what Colonel Jackson says, to show how foreign it was to the honourable nature of Sir Hudson Lowe to expect such services : " It is incumbent on me in this place distinctly to declare that Sir Hudson Lowe never breathed a word to me having reference to surveillance ; and I may also state that the great delicacy observed by him on that point first inspired in me the high respect for his character which I have never since ceased to feel up to the present moment." *

* *United Service Magazine*, March 1844, p. 418.

174

Towards people in general who visited Longwood the Governor clearly states his attitude in a letter to Sir Pulteney Malcolm, the Admiral then on the station : "When visitors did go I was not in the habit of troubling them with interrogations, and can boldly appeal to every person who has been admitted to visit at Longwood, or the Bertrands', for the delicacy I have observed on this point. I should not, however, the less expect, if anything important for me to learn was said, that it should be made known to me. If I thought reserve practised I would not hesitate to question —considering that any conversation had with General Bonaparte, or the persons of his suite, which has relation to my duties on this island, or embraces any subject of *political interest*, ought as a matter of course to be communicated to me, as well from regard to the situation I fill here as to the confidence which Government has reposed in me, being at the same time rendered by their instructions the responsible person for all conversations with him." This was an intelligible position for the Governor to maintain, and the more justifiable because of the refusal of Napoleon to hold personal intercourse with him.

(8) *That surreptitious bulletins were given to the Governor of Napoleon's health by a person who never saw him.* This charge is made by O'Meara,* and is a good example of *suppressio veri*. The explanation is simple enough. "Nothing," says Mr. Forsyth, "could be more proper than that the Governor should endeavour to obtain a second opinion as to the health and medical treatment of Napoleon from a skilful professional person, who was competent to form a judgment upon O'Meara's medical details. In reality, however, the so-called 'fictitious bulletins' were merely

* *A Voice from St. Helena*, ii. 398.

repetitions of the information given by O'Meara to Mr. Baxter, and the writer rarely expressed any opinion of his own." Dr. Baxter was the principal medical officer on the island, and his services had been offered by Sir Hudson to Napoleon, who refused to see him, and at the same time intimated that he distrusted any medical man in the confidence of the Governor. Dr. Baxter himself wrote on the subject as follows: "The expressions of Mr. O'Meara were scrupulously attended to in making the report to the Governor, and for the truth of the statements made by me to the Governor from these examinations I pledge myself as a man of honour. In the preamble to the report it is explicitly stated to be the substance of an examination of Mr. O'Meara touching the state of health of Napoleon Bonaparte, and does in no way imply that I was in attendance upon him." It is difficult to

see what there was "surreptitious" in this.
No change, however, is made in the recent
edition of O'Meara's book.

(9) *That Sir Hudson Lowe had thrown
obstacles in the way of Napoleon receiving
a marble bust of his son, the young Duc
de Reichstadt, and had even suggested that
it should be destroyed to prevent it from
reaching Longwood.* O'Meara is the principal disseminator of this charge when he
says : " The bust had been in the island
for fourteen days, during several of which
it was at Plantation House."* I have
purposely kept this charge to the last,
as it is the one that would tell (and did
tell) most of all upon the British public,
and if there had been any truth in it the
name of Sir Hudson Lowe would be
deservedly branded as that of a man
wanting in all delicacy of feeling and a
stranger to the natural affections. But

* *A Voice from St. Helena*, ii. 100, note.

the charge is simply untrue. *The bust was landed on the* 10*th or* 11*th of June and sent to Longwood on the next day.* As so much has been made of this matter, Mr. Forsyth deals with it at some length, and supports all he says by documentary evidence printed at the end of his second volume. He writes as follows: " It is not quite clear how the bust was made, but at all events it was purchased by Messrs. Beaggini in London in hopes that a favourable opportunity might occur for transmitting it to St. Helena. It happened that a vessel, the *Baring*, commanded by Captain Lamb, was about to sail there in January 1817, on board of which was a foreign sailor named Rethwick or Radovitch, in the capacity of gunner, and to him Messrs. Beaggini confided the bust, with instructions that he was to endeavour to give it to Count Bertrand for Napoleon, and to make no stipulation for any payment, but leave it to the generosity of 'the Emperor' to refund their expense. If, however, Bonaparte wished to know the price, he was to ask a hundred louis for the bust. Captain Lamb had no knowledge of the matter until shortly before or immediately after the arrival of his ship at St. Helena on May 28. At that time Rethwick was ill from a fit of apoplexy, which was succeeded by delirium, so that it was for several days impossible to speak to him on the subject. When Sir Thomas Reade was informed that the bust was on board, he immediately went to the Governor and acquainted him with the fact. Sir Hudson Lowe at first hesitated as to the course which his duty required him to take— considering the clandestine manner in which an attempt was thus made to communicate with Napoleon—and he was inclined not to allow the bust to be forwarded until he had communicated with Lord Bathurst on the subject. Sir Thomas Reade, however, suggested that, as the bust was made of marble and not plaster, so that it could not possibly contain anything improper, it might be forwarded to Longwood at once, and, as its arrival had already become known, Sir Hudson assented to the proposal. Before, however, ordering it to be sent on shore, he went on June 10 to Longwood to communicate with Count Bertrand and ascertain Napoleon's wishes. Major Gorrequer accompanied him, and he gives in his Minutes the following account of the interview:

'The Governor called on Count Bertrand (whither I attended him), and informed him that in the storeship (the *Baring*) was a marble bust said to be that of the young Napoleon; that it appeared it was brought out by an under-officer of the ship; that, although it had come in a very irregular manner, yet, under the impression that it might be a thing acceptable '*à celui qui résidait à Longwood,*' he would take upon himself the responsibility of landing it, if such was his wish; that he requested Count Bertrand would make it known, and inform him if he wished to have it, and it would be brought on shore. He answered, '*Oh! sans doute, que ça lui fera plaisir; envoyez-le toujours.*' The Governor added, the man in whose charge it came was ill, in fact delirious, and it was impossible to speak to him on the subject. All he knew about it would be found in the two papers (one a letter, the other a memorandum) which he handed over to the Count, who read them (they were in Italian) and returned them. After leaving the house, the Governor went back (I following), and again gave the two papers to the Count, that he might show them to General Bonaparte, begging he afterwards would return them to him, and told Count Bertrand he would have the bust landed the following day.'

"The next day the bust was landed and sent up to Longwood, when Bonaparte received it with evident satisfaction and delight. He had, however, been informed of its arrival (how it does not appear) some days previously. On the 10th he had said to O'Meara : 'I have known of it for several days. I intended, if it had not been given, to have made such a complaint as would have caused every Englishman's hair to stand on end with horror. I would have told a tale which would have made the mothers of England execrate him as a monster in human shape.' No one can doubt this, for there was no lack of willingness or of ability for the purpose ; but unfortunately for the well-conceived plot of the story the Governor did not give him the opportunity. But Napoleon persisted in believing, or affecting to believe, that the latter had originally given orders for the destruction of the bust, telling O'Meara, who endeavoured to convince him of the contrary, 'that it was in vain to attempt to deny a known fact'; and upon this imaginary hypothesis he broke out into a violent tirade against Sir

Sir Hudson Lowe and Napoleon

Hudson Lowe, calling him barbarous
and atrocious. 'That countenance,' he
exclaimed, gazing at the marble image
of his son, 'would melt the heart of the
most ferocious wild beast. The man who
gave orders to break that image would
plunge a knife into the heart of the
original if it were in his power.'"* Subsequently Count Bertrand had an interview with Captain Lamb, and asked him
whether the Governor had not intended
to keep back the bust altogether, and
whether he had not spoken of breaking
it to pieces. To this Captain Lamb very
properly replied that if Sir Hudson Lowe
had intended to keep it back he need only
have mentioned his wish to him, when of
course it would not have been landed.
The sailor who brought it received a
cheque for £300 from the Emperor. Of
him O'Meara says: "By means of some

* Forsyth, ii. 146–149.

unworthy tricks the poor man did not receive the money for nearly two years." The fact is, however, that the man turned out to be a great scamp. He received the money and would not return any of it to Messrs. Beaggini, who, about a year and eight months afterwards, wrote to Count Bertrand to inform him of the conduct of Radovitch, and to solicit some remuneration for themselves. It will hardly be believed that this atrocious charge against Sir Hudson Lowe is retained unaltered in the 1888 edition of O'Meara's book, in spite of the exposure of its falsehood by Mr. Forsyth. At a later period Sir Hudson Lowe received a despatch from Lord Bathurst containing the Prince Regent's approval of his conduct in sending to Napoleon the bust of his son. But Lord Bathurst added : " The suspicious circumstances, however, under which it arrived at St. Helena, as detailed

in your despatch, were sufficient to make
you pause before you determined to
transmit it to the General. Had the
package contained anything less interesting to him in his private character as a
father, the clandestine manner in which
it appears to have been introduced on
board the vessel would have been a
sufficient reason for withholding the delivery of it, at least for a much longer
period." The Government therefore not
only approved of Sir Hudson Lowe's
conduct in this matter, but evidently
considered that he needed a slight warn-
ing against showing too much leniency.

The chief specific charges against Sir
Hudson Lowe have now been stated, and
it is time to look a little at the other side
of the picture, to show not merely that he
was not guilty of any of the atrocities of
which he had been so recklessly accused,
but that he was a man remarkable for

delicacy, generosity, and humanity. To
his delicacy Mr. Henry bears witness in
the following striking passage :

" It is extremely probable, and I believe it to
be a fact, that Sir Hudson Lowe went to St.
Helena determined to conduct himself with
courtesy and kindness to Napoleon, and to
afford him as many comforts and as much
personal freedom as were consistent with his
safe custody. I was intimately acquainted with
the officer charged with the care of Longwood
for nearly three years, and he assured me that
the Governor repeatedly desired him to consult
the comfort of the great man and his suite, to
attend to their suggestions, and to make their
residence as agreeable as possible. Two of the
orderly officers at Longwood, namely, Majors
Blakeney and Nicholls of the 66th Regiment,
have given me the same assurance. I have
myself seen courteous notes from Sir Hudson
Lowe to these officers, accompanying pheasants
and other delicacies sent from Plantation House
for Napoleon's table. Even after two unfortunate interviews, when the Emperor worked himself into a rage and used gross and insulting
expressions to the Governor, evidently to put

him into a passion, but without success (for Sir
Hudson maintained perfect self-possession and
self-command throughout), even after this open
breach the above civilities were not discontinued.
Still, when a pheasant, the greatest rarity in the
island, appeared on the Governor's table, one
was sure to be sent to Longwood." *

A little further on the same writer says :

"During my residence at St. Helena opportunities of observing minutely the character of
Sir Hudson Lowe were not wanting, and I
believe nobody could fill all the ordinary relations of domestic life and of society better than
this much calumniated man. He was to my
certain knowledge a kind husband and father,
and I believe an excellent magistrate and civil
governor."

I have mentioned acts of courtesy on
the part of Sir Hudson Lowe to Countess
Bertrand. There was no reason to com-
plain of her demeanour or of that of
Countess Montholon during their stay at
St. Helena. Countess Bertrand was a

* Henry, ii. 57.

lady of much spirit and wit. Mr. Henry frequently lets us see how highly he thought of her. One of her witty remarks is preserved amid the constant tale of bickering. She was confined in January 1817, and some days afterwards, when Napoleon paid her a visit, she said to him : " Sire, I have the honour to present to your Majesty *le premier Français* who, since your arrival, has entered Longwood without Lord Bathurst's permission." The child was named after the Emperors of Austria and Russia and the Duke of Wellington. When a letter arrived announcing the death of the Countess's mother, Sir Hudson Lowe sent it with a note to Count Bertrand from himself, so that the news might be broken gently to her. No one could have acted with more delicacy ; yet because, nearly a year afterwards, the Countess received a letter brought by a person who came out as

governess to her children, speaking of
the death of her mother as a long past
event, he is, under the head of " Brutal
conduct of Sir Hudson Lowe to the
Countess Bertrand," accused by O'Meara
of little less than a design upon her life
in having suffered the letter to reach her ! *
Again, when a newspaper arrived which
contained an announcement that Count
Bertrand had been condemned *par con-
tumace* for high treason, Sir Hudson
Lowe caused the paper to be sent
separately to the Count with a private
note, for fear the news might first meet
the eye of the Countess.   At another time,
when a newspaper mentioned the death of
one of Count Montholon's children, the
Governor enclosed the paper with a note
to the Abbé Buonavita, whom he con-

* O'Meara's *Exposition*, pp. 152, 153.   This was a
publication sent out by O'Meara to St. Helena in 1819 : a
sort of skeleton outline, afterwards filled out to the proportions of *A Voice from St. Helena.*

sidered the proper person to break the information to Count Montholon. These are indeed remarkable instances of coarse-mindedness and brutality on the Governor's part! Let it be noticed also how some of his civilities were received. Early in July 1817 there arrived at St. Helena a beautiful set of chessmen, two workboxes, and some other articles of Chinese manufacture as a present to Napoleon from the Hon. John Elphinstone, as a mark of gratitude to the Emperor for having saved the life of his brother, Captain Elphinstone, who was severely wounded and made prisoner on the day before Waterloo. Mr. Forsyth thus writes : " The letter that accompanied them was immediately forwarded to Long-wood, with an intimation that the articles would follow. On examining them it was discovered that the presents were marked with eagles and the initial N., surmounted by the Imperial crown, a recognition or allusion to his former rank which rendered them under the regulations inadmissible. Sir Hudson Lowe, however, did not enforce the rules, and transmitted the articles ; but he thought it right to advert to the irregularity, and wrote to Bertrand, saying that if he were to act in strict conformity with the established rules he ought to delay sending them ; but that, as he had promised that the boxes should follow the letter, he had no alternative but to forward them." Bertrand replied angrily that the Emperor would not accept favours from anybody, nor be indebted for anything to the caprice of any one, but that he claimed to be made acquainted with the restrictions imposed upon him." Sir Hudson answered : " I have not the pretension to bestow a favour on General Bonaparte, and still less the arrogance of subjecting him to any act of my caprice. He is under no restriction which my Government does not know, and which all the world may not know." Some time afterwards Lord Bathurst wrote to Sir Hudson Lowe that the Government, while approving of the Governor's having forwarded the presents to Napoleon under the circumstances, yet "in case of any present being hereafter forwarded to General Bonaparte to which emblems or titles of sovereignty are annexed, you are to consider that circumstance as altogether precluding its delivery, if they cannot be removed without prejudice to the present itself." It may be granted that this attitude is undignified and altogether unworthy of the British Government ; but, as before remarked, the point to insist on is that Sir Hudson Lowe used his power to mitigate harshness and not to aggravate it. We come across another of O'Meara's misstatements in connexion with these very presents. He says that Captain Haviside, who brought them from China, "on having obtained permission to visit Longwood soon after his arrival, was ordered by the Governor to maintain a strict silence on the subject to all the French."* Years afterwards, on reading the passage in O'Meara's book, Captain Haviside spontaneously wrote to Sir Hudson Lowe, saying he trusted Sir Hudson would do him the honour to believe that he was not the author of this misrepresentation, that he had had every facility given him for visiting Longwood, and that he conversed some time with Count and Countess Bertrand on the subject of the presents. And yet the misrepresentation is repeated in the recent edition of O'Meara, no notice whatever being taken of Captain Haviside's contradiction! Soon after his arrival at St. Helena Sir Hudson Lowe sent up some fowling-pieces to Longwood. This was

* *A Voice from St. Helena*, ii. 118.

resented as an insult, on the ground that the parts of the island where game could be shot were outside the precincts of Longwood ; and yet at another time the servant Santini boasted that he supplied the table with the game he shot, when it was wished to make out that they were short of provisions! A writer in the *Leisure Hour* shall give another instance: "A wish on one occasion was expressed for a set of dining-tables. Immediately, as in every instance of the kind, no labour attainable on the island, and indeed no expense, was spared in order as expeditiously as possible to meet the requirements, and in a very short time a handsome mahogany set made its appearance at Longwood. When seeing it, one of the Emperor's most distinguished attendants gave orders for its removal, observing at the same time that it was not at all the thing the Emperor desired; he wished for a plain deal table. Promptly, as before, was this wish also met, and a deal table accordingly was placed by direction in one of the dining-rooms at Longwood. On one occasion some visitors were conducted over several of the apartments, not excepting the dining-room referred to, with the deal table. The strangers, beholding the Emperor's humble dining-table, as intimated to them by their polite attendant with an expressive shrug, were at once overwhelmed with amazement and the deepest sympathy."* On their return to England, these people, with the best intentions, naturally gave this as an instance of the affronts and privations endured by the illustrious exile. Sir Hudson Lowe sent some excellent coffee to Longwood, thinking it would be an acceptable present. And so it was considered by Napoleon;

* *Leisure Hour*, October 1, 1870, "Recollections of St. Helena."

but Count Montholon called it "an inexplicable idea of performing an act of politeness," and hesitated to convey the message about it to Napoleon, who, however, said to his astonishment : "Cause the case to be carried to the pantry ; good coffee is a precious thing in this horrible place." Cipriani, the *maître-d'hôtel*, suspected that the coffee might be *poisoned !* Montholon adds, "in fact, the coffee was excellent." During the February of 1821 (about two months before his death) Napoleon was attacked with constant sickness, and had great difficulty in keeping any food upon his stomach. Meat jelly made of veal was what he most easily retained, and when this was discovered some was immediately sent for his use from Plantation House, and a cook was also despatched by the Governor to Longwood who made excellent soup, of which Napoleon partook with much en-

Sir Hudson Lowe and Napoleon

joyment. Count Montholon told Captain Lutyens (the orderly officer) "it was so good the d——d doctor would not let the Emperor eat much of it." We read also of the Governor sending books from his own library of the kind which Napoleon said he wanted, and he desired his secretary to make it known that he would attend to any further suggestions on the same subject. But perhaps enough has been said of the peculiar "brutality" of Sir Hudson Lowe. His generosity towards General Gourgaud has already been mentioned. Another striking instance is supplied by Mr. Henry, who says:

> "When about to quit St. Helena, some of the foreigners were found to be considerably in debt to the shopkeepers in James Town, and one of the highest rank among them owed no less a sum than between nine hundred and a thousand pounds. Payment being delayed, legal measures were threatened, and all was consternation at Longwood. In this dilemma application was

198

made to the Governor, who handsomely offered to guarantee payment of the debt, thus removing the principal difficulty in the way of their embarkation. I have heard that the amount was paid soon after their arrival in Europe, and I should expect nothing else from the high character of the distinguished debtor. This generous behaviour of the Governor, together with other acts of kindness to the exiles, after Napoleon's death, notwithstanding the abuse they had all publicly and privately showered upon his character, prove that Sir Hudson Lowe was a very different man from what he was represented by his enemies at the time, and what the world still believes him to be."[*]

Many years later one of the atrocious calumnies circulated against Sir Hudson Lowe was this : A paragraph appeared in a London paper stating (as a quotation from the *National*) that military executions were more frequent in Sicily then than they had been since the time that Sir Hudson Lowe held an appointment there. Sir Hudson Lowe wrote to the editor as

[*] Henry, ii. 87.

follows : " I feel impelled to address this note to you to desire it may be understood that I never was employed as British Agent at the Neapolitan Court, and that I utterly deny the existence of a single circumstance of any description or import which can justify any person in presuming to couple my name with military trials or executions in Sicily or any other quarter of the globe." And yet, after all, Sir Hudson Lowe's name had been connected with military executions in Calabria. But how? In an attempt to put a stop to them, as has already been mentioned, when he wrote to General Berthier thirty years earlier. Does not this well illustrate Sir Hudson's own remark that whatever kindness he " was guilty of " was turned against him?

His humanity was shown on a larger scale by a measure which has attracted little attention, but which links the name of Sir Hudson Lowe most honourably with the island of St. Helena. In 1818 he obtained the consent of the slave proprietors, not without some difficulty, to abolish slavery without receiving any compensation. It was resolved at a meeting of the chief proprietors, "that from and after the 25th December next ensuing all children born of slaves shall be considered free." Thus the abolition was unattended with expense, and the mischief of sudden emancipation avoided. Sir Hudson Lowe's skill and management on this occasion were highly appreciated by the East India Company, who thus cleared all their possessions from this institution. In reference to this measure at St. Helena, Sir Thomas Fowell Buxton is reported as having spoken as follows in the House of Commons on the May 15, 1823:

> "The extinction of slavery which he declared to be his object was to be effected by ordaining that all negro children born after a certain day

should be free. Now, he would put it to his
opponents, where did they find this in their view
necessarily noisy [*sic; qy.* noxious] principle at
work? It is in full operation at this time at
St. Helena. Public curiosity has recently been
excited in an extraordinary degree. Books
enough have been written to fill a library detail-
ing the administration of Sir Hudson Lowe.
Acts the most slight, anecdotes the most trivial,
expressions the most unmeaning have been
recorded with exact fidelity. Generations not
yet born shall know that on such a day in July
Sir Hudson Lowe pronounced that the weather
was warm, and that on such a day in the following December Bonaparte offered a conjecture
that it would rain in the course of a week.
Nothing has escaped the researches of the
historian. Nothing has been overlooked by the
curiosity of the public. *Nothing?* Yes, one
thing has never been noticed. It has never
been noticed that Sir Hudson Lowe gave the
deathblow to slavery on that island."

Napoleon died on the evening of May 5,
1821. On that day the Governor went
early to Longwood, stayed there the
whole day, and did not return until all was

over. Mr. Henry gives an interesting account of what followed :

> " The important event of the day was naturally the chief topic of conversation in the evening, as Sir Hudson took a hurried dinner, previous to writing his despatches; and, in bare justice to an ill-used man, I can testify that, notwithstanding the bitter passages between the great departed and himself, the Governor spoke of him in a feeling, respectful and most proper manner. Major Gorrequer (the Military Secretary), Sir Hudson and myself, walked for a short time before the door of Plantation House, conversing on the character of the deceased. One of us remarked that he was the greatest enemy England ever had. 'Well, gentlemen,' said the Governor, 'he was England's greatest enemy, and mine too, but I forgive him everything. On the death of a great man like him, we should only feel deep concern and regret.'" *

On the next day Sir Hudson Lowe wrote to Lady Holland : " The compassionate interest which your Ladyship has so constantly and in so generous a manner

* Henry ii. 80.

shown towards the remarkable person who has been so long under my care, impresses it as a duty on me to take the earliest opportunity of informing you that he breathed his last yesterday evening at about ten minutes before six o'clock."

On the death of Napoleon the whole importance of Sir Hudson Lowe's employment vanished. The unpopularity of having been charged with that employment alone awaited him.

CHAPTER IV

AFTER ST. HELENA

SIR HUDSON LOWE left St. Helena at the end of July. Before his arrival in England Lord Bathurst had written a despatch conveying to him the King's marked approbation of his conduct during the whole period of his government at St. Helena. Sir Hudson Lowe was presented to the King on November 14 ; and, when he was about to kiss His Majesty's hand, the King took hold of his and shook it heartily, saying : " I congratulate you most sincerely upon your return, after a trial the most arduous and exemplary that perhaps any man ever had. I have felt for your situation, and may appeal to Lord Bathurst how frequently I have talked to him about you." Soon afterwards he was appointed to the first vacant colonelcy of a regiment (the 93rd) that occurred after his return to England.

But evil days were at hand. In July 1822 came out O'Meara's *A Voice from St. Helena*, and the sensation it produced is well described by Sir Hudson Lowe himself. "Public curiosity flew with eagerness to the repast; nothing was wanting to satisfy the cravings of the most credulous, the most inquisitive, or the most malignant mind. The highest authorities were not spared; but *I* was destined to be the real victim, upon whom the public indignation was to fall."

Upon this Sir Hudson Lowe resolved to have recourse to the law for redress, and the result was an application to the Court of King's Bench for a criminal infor-

mation against O'Meara. Much time was
consumed in selecting the most libellous
passages from the book. The difficulty of
this task was great, owing to the peculiar
art with which it was composed and the
studied care taken to avoid any direct
accusation in points where any living testimony could be referred to. Time was,
however, of the last importance, although
Sir Hudson was not aware of it. It was
not until the latter end of Hilary Term,
1823—*i.e.*, towards the end of the second
term after the publication of the libel—that
a rule *nisi* was applied for, and then it was
hinted by the Lord Chief Justice that the
application was likely to be fruitless, simply
on the technical ground that it was too late.
And so it proved, for when O'Meara's
counsel showed cause against the rule
being made absolute, he urged the fatal
objection that it was out of time, without
attempting to enter into the merits, and

this objection was upheld. It is certainly very strange that the eminent counsel who advised Sir Hudson Lowe should not have informed him of this risk. Sir Hudson next consulted his legal advisers as to the expediency of indicting O'Meara, or of bringing an action for damages; but his counsel (Mr. Tindal) said with perfect truth that the proper legal remedy had been already resorted to for the vindication of his character. He had cleared himself from every charge upon his oath, and if O'Meara challenged the truth of his denials he might test them by prosecuting Sir Hudson Lowe for perjury. But to assume that a man's character is cleared in any way by the refusal of a libeller to go on to prosecute for perjury is a notion that would occur to no one but a lawyer. It leaves the game entirely in the libeller's hands. An indictment, however, would not put in issue the truth or falsehood of the accusations contained in the libel, for Lord Campbell's Act was not then in existence. As to a civil action, it would be useless to incur the risk of obtaining only small damages, which would in reality be a triumph for the defendant. In fact, Sir Hudson Lowe's legal remedy was gone owing to the fatal delay. There was only one course now to be pursued, and another fatal mistake was made in not pursuing it. Sir Hudson Lowe should at once have vindicated his character by the publication of a complete account of his Governorship, for which he had the amplest materials, and the result could not have failed to redound to his public credit. Lord Bathurst, who was always his friend, strongly urged Sir Hudson Lowe to take this obvious course, and offered to place all the state documents at his disposal. His continued silence could not fail to impress the public unfavourably. However innocent a man may be, he cannot allow the foulest charges to be brought against him and expect no one will believe them. In Jupiter or Saturn things may be arranged differently, but here the world judges, rightly or wrongly, that a man who does nothing to vindicate his character, when it has been publicly aspersed, does not do so because he cannot do so ; and in ninety-nine cases out of a hundred the world's judgment is correct. But Sir Hudson Lowe's happened to be the hundredth case, and it cannot be denied that his failure to do what his position demanded brought on himself a penalty which he kept on suffering to the end of his life, and from which his memory still suffers. We cannot be surprised that Sir Hudson Lowe's enemies made the most of his unaccountable silence. It is therefore most material to consider why he did not follow the advice of Lord Bathurst and the rest of his friends. A man may, it is true, despise the opinion of the world and

take no heed of calumny, either because
he has a contempt for his fellow-creatures
or from a motive of religion. But Sir
Hudson Lowe was neither a cynic nor a
saint. He lived for this world, and promotion in his profession naturally depended
to a large extent on his retaining the good
opinion of the world. To complain of
calumnies, and yet to neglect the only steps
by which they can be abated, shows a
certain amount of wrong-headedness, for
which it is difficult to account completely.
However, some of the reasons by which
the ex-Governor was actuated in refusing
to make an appeal to public opinion may
be conjectured. The scruples that stood
in his way are all those of a high-minded
man, but they do more honour to his heart
than to his head. First, then, Sir Hudson
Lowe despised his enemies, more especially
O'Meara. That individual was certainly
worthy of all the contempt which the ex-

Governor felt for him ; but then the public
did not know what Sir Hudson knew, and
it is simply a blunder to despise an adver-
sary who assumes to bring forward *facts*
and not merely his own *opinions*. Such
alleged facts, by whomsoever stated, must
be shown to be untrue. The consciousness
of having honourably discharged a difficult
duty does not, as Mr. Forsyth well remarks,
"inspire enthusiasm in others, or cause
friends to cluster round the object of
calumny and reproach." Secondly, Sir
Hudson Lowe thought that, as his conduct
had been heartily approved by the King
and Government, it was rather for the
latter than for himself to undertake his
defence. But surely this was expecting
too much. A body of men like a Government can never act with the generosity of
an individual. They have seldom time or
inclination to vindicate the character of a
servant, unless their own stability is so

much bound up with that servant as to make his defence practically the same as their own. This was not the case here. It would not be too much to say that the opposite of this was the case. If a Government cannot be as generous as an individual, it can, as a body, act with a meanness of which most individuals would be ashamed, and at this time the Government by sacrificing Sir Hudson Lowe strengthened their own position, and to a large extent took the wind from the sails of the Opposition. When they were attacked for their ill-treatment of Napoleon they could tacitly transfer the odium of it to Sir Hudson Lowe, for Mr. Forsyth puts it too mildly when he says : "The Government ought to have aided Sir Hudson Lowe more heartily and effectually than they did." In the third place, and probably this weighed most of all with the chivalrous nature of Sir Hudson, who was intensely loyal to his King and country, he clearly perceived that he could not thoroughly defend himself without disclosing the shabby manner in which he had been treated by the Government during his term of office at St. Helena. He knew that O'Meara's correspondence had been encouraged by Cabinet Ministers, and that intrigues behind his back had, to say the least, not been discouraged. But I have already dealt with this topic, and need not repeat my words. It is evident that Sir Hudson Lowe acutely felt the delicacy of his position. But surely all his scruples should have been set at rest by the strongly-urged advice of Lord Bathurst to publish—Lord Bathurst, who was himself one of the principal members of the Cabinet, and who knew more about St. Helena than all the rest.

As a matter of fact, after the return of Sir Hudson Lowe nothing was ever done for him by the Government at all adequate to his merits. He certainly received from them plenty of empty praise, but *probitas laudatur et alget* ("honour is praised and —left out in the cold"), for, while those who had served under him at St. Helena were promoted on *his* recommendation, nothing was done for himself. Before he ever went to St. Helena he had been formally assured that Lord Liverpool had said that, if he went, "it should not stop there." Sir Hudson Lowe was then advised by a friend of some experience to stipulate for a pension before he went out, but he did not follow the suggestion. He felt too confident of the principles upon which he should discharge the duty in-trusted to him not to be assured that recompense must follow. The employ-ment was therefore accepted uncondi-tionally and without his seeking to establish any condition.* Colonel Wilks,

* See " Memoir," *United Service Magazine*, June 1844 p. 290.

his predecessor at St. Helena, was in
receipt of a pension of £1500. Sir
Hudson Lowe had no pension given to
him. It is said that Lord Liverpool was
prejudiced against him. The calumnies
of O'Meara may indeed have had this
effect. The writer of Sir Hudson Lowe's
life in the *Dictionary of National Biography* says: " The amount of his salary
(£12,000 a year) was specially fixed, and
no stipulation was made as to pension,
which explains the fact, upon which his
enemies remarked, that he was not afterwards considered eligible for a pension."
But surely this must be an error, or Sir
Hudson Lowe would not so persistently
have urged his claim to a pension, and we
never find that the obvious reply that he
was not eligible for one was made, but
only that if it was submitted to the House
of Commons they would not grant it.
The Government no doubt must have

felt that they had not treated Sir Hudson
Lowe fairly, and when the storm burst
upon his head they were not inclined to
help him, for the vigorous lines of Dryden
are ever true :

" Forgiveness to the injured doth belong,
But they ne'er pardon who have done the wrong."

Another disadvantage under which Sir
Hudson Lowe laboured was that he knew
so few people in England at the time.
All his active military life, previous to his
departure for St. Helena, had been spent
in Continental service, and most of the
friends he then made were now dead.
Lord Bathurst offered him in 1824 the
government of the island of Antigua (a post
ridiculously below his merits), but family
reasons prevented him from accepting it.
He was in the following year appointed
to the command of the forces in Ceylon
with a promise of the reversion of the
Governorship. Again ill-luck followed

him. The Governorship fell vacant near the end of 1830, a very short time after Earl Grey had become Prime Minister. All hope of public employment was now over for the time, for, as Mr. Forsyth remarks, "neither Earl Grey nor his colleagues could be expected to sympathise much with the former guardian of Napoleon's person, of whom it had been so long the fashion of their party to speak as the inhuman jailer of an injured prisoner."

Sir Hudson Lowe's military command in Ceylon terminated with his promotion to the rank of Lieutenant-General in 1830 (in St. Helena he held this only as a local rank), and after his return to England in 1831 he was incessantly occupied in petitioning—one might almost say pestering—the Government for some office in recognition of his services, not merely on account of his private means, which had become much reduced, but also as some answer to the calumnies against him so industriously circulated. But calumny and uncontradicted lies had at last done their natural work. Some of the mud so copiously thrown had stuck, and stuck effectually. In a memorial drawn up in 1843 Sir Hudson Lowe writes, after alluding to the state of inactivity in which he had been kept for twelve years: "The government of the island of Ceylon had thrice fallen vacant, and the chief authority in the Ionian Islands (where my local services at their liberation and in the discharge of *civil* and military duties subsequently had contributed to form a strong claim for re-employment) four times, during the period of which I have been speaking. Vacancies had also arisen in other stations. But on none of these occasions were either my local or general services, or any claim arising from past disappointment, taken into that consideration which I should have hoped might have been deemed to be their due." But it was not all gloom. Even the malice of his foes gave occasion to the championship of friends who were above the influence of party spirit. In 1833 Lord Teynham made an attack on Sir Hudson Lowe in the House of Lords. Speaking of the government of Ireland, he said, in reference to a proposal to intrust special powers to the Lord-Lieutenant (the Marquis of Normanby) : "Now suppose the noble Marquis were to be succeeded in the government of Ireland by a Sir Hudson Lowe." Here he was called to order, and when he had sat down the Duke of Wellington rose, and asking what the noble Lord meant, said : " I have the honour to know Sir Hudson Lowe, and I will say, in this House or elsewhere, wherever it may be, that there

is not in the army a more respectable
officer than Sir Hudson Lowe, nor has
His Majesty a more faithful subject." A
day or two afterwards Lord Teynham
made an abject apology, and in reply to
a letter of thanks from Sir Hudson Lowe
to the Duke for his prompt and generous
defence, the latter wrote as follows :

"STRATHFIELDSAYE, *Feb*. 21, 1833.

"MY DEAR GENERAL,—I have received your
letter of the 20th. I assure you that I considered that I did no more than my duty upon
the occasion to which you refer in repelling a
very gross and marked insinuation against an
officer, in his absence, for whom I entertained
the highest respect and regard. The discussion
ended in a way that must be highly satisfactory
to all your friends.—Ever, my dear General,
yours most faithfully,   WELLINGTON.

" Lieut.-General Sir Hudson Lowe."

In 1842 Sir Hudson Lowe was much
gratified by his transfer from the colonelcy
of the 56th to that of his old regiment, the
50th, the regiment in which he had first

received a commission. In the same year
the King of Prussia advanced him to the
First Class of the Red Eagle of Prussia,
notified in a flattering letter from Baron
von Bülow, who recalled his " signal
services to the common cause in the
glorious campaigns of 1813-14."* He
was also made a G.C.M.G., an order
which at that time was confined to those
who had rendered service in connexion
with Malta or the Ionian Islands. We have
already said that none of the French exiles
bore any ill-will towards Sir Hudson Lowe
except the Las Cases, father and son. One
day in November 1822, young Las Cases,
who was then in London, assaulted Sir
Hudson Lowe in the street, and afterwards sent him a challenge, which Sir
Hudson had the good sense and moral
courage to treat with the contempt it
deserved. Another extraordinary inci-

* *Dictionary of National Biography*, vol. xxxiv. p. 193.

dent connected with the same individual
occurred in 1825. Sir Hudson Lowe, as
may be gathered from what is already
written, was a man of the highest physical
as well as moral courage. Thus, in April
1814, when he made a journey to England
to announce the fall of Paris (a service
which Lord Cathcart regarded as perilous
in the extreme) he rode from Paris to
Calais attended by a single Cossack.
So again in 1825, when on his way to
Ceylon, disregarding the advice of friends,
he determined to pass through Paris. It
seems that while Sir Hudson was approaching Paris in his carriage young
Las Cases was found wounded near a
spot by which Sir Hudson passed, and
it was reported that an attempt had
been made by Sir Hudson Lowe to
assassinate him! The *Times* commented
upon the rumour as follows : " Our readers
will see in our French letter a curious

result drawn from the supposed attempt to assassinate young Las Cases. Sir Hudson Lowe, lately at Paris, and now on his way home,* is charged with that attempt. We expected that such would be the case; and it was by mere chance that we did not make an observation to that effect when we inserted the paragraph with the rumour of the assassination. We have not the least doubt but that the whole is a plot against Sir Hudson. Some people will say that he might as well have kept away from Paris, unless he had urgent business there; others, that he did right to show himself, in the consciousness of an innocent heart and the pride of having done his duty. We shall not decide upon this point. We thought that the journey to Paris exposed Sir Hudson to some risk,

* This was a mistake. He was on his way to Ceylon at this time.

without knowing of what kind the risk
might be. The moment we heard the
assassination story, we saw in what
way the Bonapartists were going to
work."*

The hoax was rather too palpable, and
nothing more was heard of it. On the
same journey Sir Hudson Lowe gave a
conspicuous example of his generosity.
While he was at Smyrna, and dining on
board H.M.S. *Cambrian* with Captain
Hamilton, the Secretary of the French
Consul proceeded to Sir Hudson Lowe's
lodgings with the avowed intention of
assassinating him. Not finding him in,
this worthy destroyed some of Sir Hudson's
property, and prepared to lie in wait for
his return, calling upon a friend to be
"witness of the revenge he was about
to take on the murderer and poisoner
of Napoleon." From doing this, however,

* *Times*, November 19, 1825.

he was prevented, and the matter becoming known, the French Consul dismissed the man from his employment. Sir Hudson Lowe, on receiving an assurance that he should be no further molested, and learning that his would-be assailant had a large family dependent upon him for support, wrote that "he had no desire to take any further steps in the affair, or to stand in the way of any act of lenity or consideration which the French Consul himself might think fit to show towards him."* Such then was the vindictive spirit exhibited by the "murderer and poisoner" of Napoleon.

It is pleasing to record, on the authority of his eldest son, that in spite of all his troubles Sir Hudson Lowe was never depressed. "This frame of mind appeared to be one of which he was always incapable. Up to his final seizure

* From an unpublished letter.

with paralysis he had always abundant
animal spirits. To say that he retained
his activity of mind and body and his
industry to the last would be inappro-
priate, as they may be rather considered
as having been too great for his strength." *
Most men would have become embittered
or morose under the long persecution of
which Sir Hudson Lowe was the victim.
He died in January 1844 in comparative
poverty. Sir Robert Peel recommended
Miss Lowe, his unmarried daughter, to
the Queen for a small pension which at
the time was at his disposal, "in recognition of the services of her father." This
lady still survives to cherish the memory
of a father whose domestic virtues have
never been questioned by his bitterest
assailants.

Such, then, was the career of Sir

* "Memoir," *United Service Magazine*, June 1844,
p. 294.

Sir Hudson Lowe and Napoleon

Hudson Lowe, a man of unstained honour, of undaunted courage, of unflinching resolution. He was as much devoted to duty as the Duke of Wellington. With the latter "the path of duty was the way to glory." With Sir Hudson Lowe this was not the case; but, after all, there may be better things than "glory." Sir Hudson Lowe has been the most calumniated man of this—perhaps of any—century. He has been charged with giving way to ungovernable bursts of temper; Napoleon complained that he could not make him lose his temper. He has been charged with want of courtesy; all Napoleon could say against him was that on one occasion, after being assailed with a torrent of abuse, he actually forgot himself so far as to retire rather abruptly and without the customary bow! He has been charged with want of delicacy; if he had been less delicate he would have

vindicated himself with more success.
He has been charged with brutality and
harshness in the discharge of his duty; the
only official hint of disapproval that he
ever received from the Government was
on account of his leniency. It is said
there was persecution at St. Helena; it
is true, but Sir Hudson Lowe was the
victim of it, not Napoleon. The following
words of a military writer contain no
exaggeration :

"To have been charged with an amount of
responsibility from which most men would have
shrunk aghast ; to have performed a painful duty
with sleepless vigilance ; to have been exposed
from circumstances not of his own seeking to an
amount of obloquy almost without parallel in the
annals of party; to have firmly carried out what
he had reluctantly undertaken—the safe custody
of a baffled tyrant; to have 'obeyed instructions,' and then to have been rewarded by
coolness and neglect when he might have
expected cordiality and praise, seems a hard
destiny. It was that of Sir Hudson Lowe."

Sir Hudson Lowe and Napoleon

It is to the honour of England that the truth of this miserable affair should be known, and the more widely it is known the more will it become recognised that Englishmen have no cause to be ashamed of the conduct of Sir Hudson Lowe at St. Helena.

1815. Oct. 15. Arrival of Rear-Admiral Sir George Cockburn on board the *Northumberland*, conveying Napoleon and his suite, including the surgeon, O'Meara.

1816. April 14. Arrival of Sir Hudson Lowe and suite.

   ,, 16. First interview between Napoleon and Sir Hudson Lowe.

   ,, 30. Second interview.

May 17. Third interview.

June 17. Arrival of Rear-Admiral Sir Pulteney Malcolm on board the *Newcastle* frigate, to succeed Sir George Cockburn in command of the naval station at St. Helena; also of the three foreign Commissioners.

July 17. Fourth interview.

Chronological Table

1816. Aug. 18. Fifth and last interview.
    Dec. 30. Departure of Las Cases and his son.
1818. March 14. Departure of General Gourgaud.
    Aug. 2. Departure of O'Meara.
1821. May 5. Death of Napoleon.
    July 25. Departure of Sir Hudson Lowe.

BIBLIOGRAPHY

(The following list does not claim to be exhaustive.)

1. "Letters written on board the *Northumberland* and at St. Helena, on Napoleon and his Suite." By William Warden. London, 1816. 8vo.

2. "Manuscrit venu de Ste. Hélène d'une manière inconnue."* 2 vols. London, 1817. 8vo.

3. "An Appeal to the British Nation on the Treatment experienced by Napoleon Bonaparte in the Island of St. Helena." By M. Santini, Porter of the Emperor's Closet. London, 1816. [This pamphlet was really by Colonel Maceroni.]

4. "Letters from the Cape of Good Hope, in reply to Mr. Warden." 1817. [By O'Meara.]

5. "Mémoires de E. A. D. Comte de Las Casas." Bruxelles, 1818. 8vo.

6. The same, translated into English. London, 1818. 8vo.

* By some attributed to Napoleon, but really by M. Lullin de Chateauvieux.

† So spelt in the titles of his books.

Bibliography

7. "Facts illustrative of the Treatment of Napoleon Bonaparte." By T. E. H. [Theodore Hook]. London, 1819. 8vo.

8. "An Exposition of some of the Transactions that have taken place at St. Helena since the appointment of Sir Hudson Lowe as Governor of that Island." By B. E. O'Meara. London, 1819. 8vo.

9. "Napoleon in Exile: or, A Voice from St. Helena." By Barry E. O'Meara, Esq., his late Surgeon. 2 vols. London, 1822. 8vo.

10. "Mémorial de Ste. Hélène: Journal de la vie privée et des conversations de l'Empereur Napoléon à Ste. Hélène." Par le Comte de Las Casas. 4 tom. Londres, 1823. 8vo.

11. The same, translated into English. 4 vols. London, 1823. 8vo.

12. "Derniers Momens de Napoléon." Par C. F. Antommarchi. 2 tom. Paris et Londres, 1825. 8vo.

13. The same, translated into English. 2 vols. London, 1825. 8vo.

14. "Life of Napoleon Bonaparte." By Sir Walter Scott. 9 vols. London, 1827. 8vo.

15. "Buonaparte's Voyage to St. Helena, comprising the Diary of Sir George Cockburn during his passage from England to St. Helena in 1815." Boston [Mass.], 1833. 12mo.

16. The same, with a Preface by T. S. Borradaile, London, 1888. 8vo.

17. "Events of a Military Life." By Walter Henry, Surgeon to the Forces. First class. Second Edition. 2 vols. London, 1843. [Vol. ii., pp. 1–97 have reference to St. Helena.]

18. "Recollections of the Emperor Napoleon during the first three years of his captivity on the island of St. Helena." By L. E. Abell.* London, 1844. 12mo.

19. Third edition of the same, revised and added to by Mrs. C. Johnston. London, 1873. 8vo.

20. " Récits de la Captivité de l'Empereur Napoléon à Ste. Hélène. Par C. J. F. T. de Montholon, Marquis de Montholon-Sémonville. 2 tom. Paris, 1847. 8vo.

21. The same, translated into English. 4 vols. London, 1846–1847. 8vo.

22. "History of the Captivity of Napoleon at St. Helena; from the Letters and Journals of the late Lieut.-General Sir Hudson Lowe, and Official Documents not before made public." By William Forsyth, M.A. 3 vols. London, 1853. 8vo.

23. "Notes and Reminiscences of a Staff Officer, chiefly relating to the Waterloo Campaign and to St. Helena matters during the Captivity of Napoleon." By Lieut.-Colonel Basil Jackson. [Printed for private circulation.] London, 1877. 8vo.

* Mrs. Abell, formerly Miss Elizabeth Balcombe.

Bibliography

24. "Berichte aus St. Helena zur Internirung
    Napoleon Bonaparte's." Von B. F. v.
    Stürmer, herausg. V. H. Schlitter. Wien,
    1886. 8vo.

25. "Napoleon at St. Helena." By Barry Edward
    O'Meara, his late Surgeon. 2 vols. London,
    1888. 8vo. [A reprint of " A Voice from
    St. Helena," with certain additions and
    omissions.]

26. "La Captivité de Ste. Hélène d'après les rap-
    ports inédits du Marquis de Montchenu."
    Par Georges Firmin Didot. Paris, 1894,
    8vo.

27. "United Service Magazine." October and
    November, 1843 ; March–June, 1844.

28. "Quarterly Review." Nos. 31 (Oct. 1816),
    32 (Jan. 1817), 34 (July 1817), 55 (Oct.
    1822), 65 (Dec. 1825).

29. "Edinburgh Review." Nos. 59 (Dec. 1816),
    73 (June 1822), 76 (May 1823).

THE END

Printed by BALLANTYNE, HANSON & Co.
London & Edinburgh

A Selection from D. Nutt's Publications.

THE CONSTITUTION AND ADMINISTRA-
TION OF THE UNITED STATES. By
BENJAMIN HARRISON, ex-President. Crown 8vo,
xxiv., 300 pp. Cloth, 3s. 6d.

** *A popular but thoroughly authoritative exposi-
tion of the governing system of the United States.*

Some Press Notes.

"This is one of the most interesting books that has
reached us from the other side of the Atlantic for a
long time. It is neither a philosophical dissertation on
the duties of a citizen, nor a commentary on the
Constitution of the United States. It simply and
modestly lays bare the machinery of American National
Government, with the frankness only probable in an
American and the knowledge only possible in an ex-
President."—*Daily Chronicle.*

"No one can read this interesting little work without
acknowledging that ex-President Harrison shares, with
other great personages, such as the Emperor of Germany
and the late M. Thiers, the possession of the art of
ruling men united with a rare eloquence. The work is
composed of some twenty-one chapters, with an appendix
containing the written Constitution of the United
States. It is most ungrudging in its scope, ranging
from discussions of the highest constitutional questions
to familiar anecdotes about various presidents. The

two concluding chapters on the Judiciary are especially interesting. They contain 'a treasury of suggestion' for readers of no exclusive nationality."—*Law Times.*

" A book which deserves to be widely read. While Mr. Bryce's book deals with the problems of democracy in the historico-philosophical spirit, Mr. Harrison has given us a plain, practical, and matter-of-fact statement of the facts. He speaks as one who knows: he has been President for two terms, and has had much experience of the working of all the departments of Government in the States."—*Scotsman.*

ADAMS (G. B.). CIVILISATION DURING THE MIDDLE AGES, especially in relation to Modern Civilisation. Demy 8vo. 1894. viii., 473 pp. Cloth. 10s. 6d.

ENGLISH HISTORY, FROM CONTEMPORARY WRITERS. Edited by Prof. F. YORK POWELL. In 16mo volumes, averaging 200 pages, with illustrations, neatly bound in cloth, cut flush, 1s.; or cloth uncut edges, 1s. 6d., comprising extracts from the Chronicles, State Papers, and Memoirs of the time, chronologically arranged. With Introductions, Notes, accounts of authorities, Tables, Maps, Illustrations, &c.

EDWARD III. AND HIS WARS (1327–1360). Edited by W. J. ASHLEY, M.A.

THE MISRULE OF HENRY III. (1236–1251). Edited by the Rev. W. H. HUTTON, M.A.

STRONGBOW'S CONQUEST OF IRELAND. Edited by F. P. BARNARD, M.A.

SIMON OF MONTFORD AND HIS CAUSE (1251–1265). Edited by the Rev. W. H. HUTTON, M.A.

THE CRUSADE OF RICHARD I. Edited by
T. A. ARCHER. 396 pp. 2s. and 2s. 6d.

S. THOMAS OF CANTERBURY. By Rev. W.
H. HUTTON. 286 pp. 1s. 6d. and 2s.

ENGLAND UNDER CHARLES II., FROM THE
RESTORATION TO THE TREATY OF NIMWEGEN.
Edited by W. TAYLOR.

THE WARS OF THE ROSES. Edited by Miss
E. THOMPSON. 180 pp. 1892.

THE JEWS OF ANGEVIN ENGLAND. Edited
by J. JACOBS. xxix., 425 pp. 1893. 4s. and
4s. 6d.

SCOTTISH HISTORY, FROM CONTEMPORARY
WRITERS. THE DAYS OF JAMES IV. Edited by
G. GREGORY SMITH, M.A. 1891. 1s.

GUMMERE (F. B.). GERMANIC ORIGINS. A
Study in Primitive Culture. 8vo. 1892. 500 pp.
Cloth. 10s. 6d.

Contents : Land and People—Men and Women—
The Home—Husband and Wife—The Family—
Trade and Commerce—The Warrior—Social
Order—Government and Law—The Funeral—
The Worship of the Dead—The Worship of
Nature—The Worship of Gods—Form and Cere-
mony—The Higher Mood.

JACOBS (Joseph). AN INQUIRY INTO THE
SOURCES OF THE HISTORY OF THE JEWS IN
SPAIN. Demy 8vo. 1894. xlix., 263 pp.
Cloth. Nett 4s.

JACOBS (Joseph). STUDIES IN JEWISH STA-
TISTICS, Social, Vital, and Anthropometric. 8vo.
1891. viii., 59. lxix., 77–88 pp. Plans and
plates. Cloth. Nett 6s.

Contents: Consanguineous Marriages—Social Con-
ditions of the Jews in London—Occupations—
Professions—Vital Statistics—Racial Characteristics of Modern Jews—Comparative Distribution
of Jewish Ability—Comparative Anthropometry
of English Jews.

JAMES. THE SCULPTURES IN THE LADY
CHAPEL AT ELY. Illustrated in fifty-five collotype
plates. With descriptions and identifications by
MONTAGUE RHODES JAMES, and a Preface by the
Lord Bishop of the Diocese. 4to. 1895. 55
plates, 68 pp. of illustrative text. Cloth. Nett
£1 5s.

THE VOYAGES MADE BY THE SIEUR
D.B. TO THE ISLANDS DAUPHINE OR MADAGASCAR,
AND BOURBON OR MASCARENNE, IN THE YEARS
1669–72. Translated and edited by Captain
PASFIELD OLIVER (late Royal Artillery), editor of
"The Voyage of François Leguat" (Hakluyt
Edition). Medium 8vo. 1897. 176 pp. With
numerous illustrations and maps. Cloth. Nett
10s. 6d.

DAVID NUTT, 270-271 STRAND.